100 SCENIC DESCRIPTIONS FROM GREAT NOVELS

外國名著風景描寫一百段

一百叢書⑲

英漢對照English-Chinese

張合珍 選譯　張信威 編審

外國名著
風景描寫一百段
100
SCENIC
DESCRIPTIONS
FROM
GREAT NOVELS

臺 灣 商 務 印 書 館 發 行

《一百叢書》總序

本館出版英漢 (或漢英) 對照《一百叢書》的目的,是希望憑藉着英、漢兩種語言的對譯,把中國和世界各類著名作品的精華部分介紹給中外讀者。

本叢書的涉及面很廣。題材包括了寓言、詩歌、散文、短篇小説、書信、演説、語錄、神話故事、聖經故事、成語故事、名著選段等等。

顧名思義,《一百叢書》中的每一種都由一百個單元組成。以一百為單位,主要是讓編譯者在浩瀚的名著的海洋中作挑選時有一個取捨的最低和最高限額。至於取捨的標準,則是見仁見智,各有心得。

由於各種書中被選用的篇章節段,都是以原文或已被認定的範本作藍本,而譯文又經專家學者們精雕細琢,千錘百煉,故本叢書除可作為各種題材的精選讀本外,也是研習英漢兩種語言對譯的理想參考書,部分更可用作朗誦教材。外國學者如要研習漢語,本書亦不失為理想工具。

商務印書館 (香港) 有限公司
編輯部

前　言

藝術美高於自然

> ——黑格爾：《美學》

　　美是一種理想的境界，也是人類的一種崇高的追求。

　　大自然是人類的棲息地，它是一個瑰麗多姿的神奇世界。青山、翠谷、繁花、綺石，這些都是大自然的造化。萬物皆有靈，萬物都含美，這些自然風景經過藝術家們的精心雕琢，就更富有美的神韻，深深地打動着我們。熱愛大自然是人類的天性，我們煩惱時向大自然求安慰和解脫，快樂時到自然界尋找感應和共鳴。我們感情中的很大部分是大自然賦予的，因為人類與其周圍的自然界本來就是情投意合，我們對周圍美景的欣賞力都是我們的一種文明的造詣。

　　藝術家筆下的自然風景描寫是自然美、藝術美、心靈美的結晶，它源於自然，而又超乎自然，在文學作品裏，風景描寫大體有以下三種文學功能：

一、賞心悅目、怡情養性

大自然是人類的摯友，它向人們無私地奉獻着它的美，供品嘗；她那雲霧繚繞、氣象萬千的崇山峻嶺；草木青葱，生機盎然的幽谷；綠浪滾滾、一望無際的平原；奔騰不息；滔滔入海的小河大江；銀光閃爍、漣漪片片的大湖；意境深幽、野趣橫生的森林，霞光滿天，日月爭輝的蒼穹——江山多嬌，山川之美是無與倫比的，美在天氣，美在時光，美在季節的更迭。春天百花吐艷、夏天濃綠深蔭、秋天碧空薄雲、冬天白雪皚皚，無不具有觀賞價值。細細品嚐景中詩情畫意，既可休養身心，又可陶冶性情，激發內心喜悅，脫離塵囂，忘卻煩憂，何樂而不為？

二、融情於景，為故事情節營造氣氛

文學作品中，純粹作為客觀欣賞的風景描寫是很少出現的。在大多數情況下，風景描寫的文學功能，是融情於景，為故事營造氣氛，讓讀者如見其景、如聞其聲，有身臨其境之感。這樣的例子書中比比皆是。

"賽似伊甸園"描繪在蜜露降臨、萬籟俱寂的薄暮時分，在滿園青翠、花果繁茂的庭園裏信步漫遊的情景，一種閑逸之情油然而生。

"寧靜的秋日"裏遼闊的牧場依然枝繁葉茂，絢麗多姿。但小徑上颯颯飄落的黃葉和其間夾雜的一、二朵暗淡而柔弱的小花，足以宣告它的凋零之態。不禁給人一種蕭瑟、悽涼的情調。

"快活谷"描繪的是一個靜靜的美麗的自然界。這裏清流環繞，草木青翠，水聲淙淙，花兒婀娜嬌美，整個畫面，煙雨迷濛，幽美清新，充滿了濃郁的詩情畫意。景為情設，情為景生，此情此景，能不令人覺得幸福甜蜜？

凝望着火紅的太陽從西邊的蒼穹緩緩沉落，無疑是人間最美的景色之一。對《兒子與情人》中的穆萊爾太太來說，猶如對其他人一樣，這是最靜謐的時刻。在這種時刻，那些煩人的瑣事不翼而飛，美好的事物呈現在眼前，心中恢復了平靜和力量，使我們能夠重新看到自己。

"野營風光"裏的景色描繪意境深遠，是較為典型的情景反襯。夜晚微風陣陣，松濤低吟，幽暗的湖水泛着輕輕的漣漪，但是這番良辰美景不但沒有賦予《美國的悲劇》的主人公克萊德以美的愉悅，反而令他更痛苦，更難受。克萊德焦急、痛苦、憂心如焚的內心世界，在景色描寫的反襯中昭然若揭。

三、為故事提供背景

文學作品中的許多自然風景描寫是作為人物活動的場

所的。

　　本書選段"塵沙"是小說《憤怒的葡萄》開篇的一部分，它點出了故事的背景，美國西南部奧克拉荷馬地區的地域特點：雨量稀少，驕陽似火，日夜蒸烤着大地。狂風肆虐，刮起塵埃遮天蔽日，在一片矇矓的世界裏，倒伏的莊稼在呻吟、在悲鳴。整個描繪給讀者呈現出一幅貧瘠農村的淒涼景象。又如哈代的《還鄉》對愛敦荒原的精彩描繪，被認為是英國小說中為數不多的散文佳作："原來這個地方，能夠讓喜歡它的人回憶起來覺得有一種不同尋常、溫藹和諧的面貌"，"蒼蒼的暮色和愛敦荒原的景物，共同造出一種風光，堂皇而不嚴峻，感人而無粉飾，有深遠的告誡性，有渾厚的醇樸味"成千古絕唱。這番景色描寫不僅為悲劇氣氛甚濃的故事提供了背景場地，也給作品增姿添色。此外，選自笛福的《魯濱遜漂流記》的"荒島上的世外桃源"，描繪了一個夢幻般的世外桃源。但這個理想天堂卻在文明世界裏找不到，而地處於了無人煙、與世隔絕的小島上，正好就成為該小說的中心場地。

　　選材猶如選新郎，心情之殷切，期望之高，取捨之難，可想而知。古往今來，世界文學寶庫中的名著浩如煙海，對名著作品的具體界定見仁見智，似無統一依據。本書選材大體按照 Cliff Notes 封底所列的世界文學名著目錄，從知名度高的世界文學巨匠的作品中，擷取風景描寫的精彩片段，奉獻給讀者。所選的作家作品盡量多元化，包括哈代的《還鄉》、《德伯家的苔絲》、《卡斯特橋市長》，狄更斯的《大衛‧科波菲爾》、《苦海孤雛》、《遠大前程》、《老古玩店》、《荒涼山莊》，夏洛蒂‧勃朗特的《簡‧愛》，薩克雷的《名利場》，勞倫斯的《兒子與情人》，麥爾維爾的《白鯨》，霍桑的《紅字》，詹姆士的《一位女士的畫像》，劉易斯的《大街》，海明威的《太陽照常升起》、《永別了武器》，斯坦貝克的《憤怒的葡萄》，馬克‧吐溫的《湯姆‧索耶歷險記》，凱瑟的《我的安東尼亞》，托爾斯泰的《戰爭與和平》、《安娜‧卡列尼娜》，肖洛霍夫的《靜靜的頓河》，羅蘭的《約翰‧克列斯朵夫》，福樓拜的《包法利夫人》，塞萬提斯的《唐‧吉訶德》，等四十多部名著作品。除個別例外，一般每本書不超過三篇選段。

語言也是本書選材所考慮的因素之一，在浩瀚的文學海洋中，本書選材確定以英、美文學名著為主，其他歐洲文學名著為輔的原則。最佳的選材，不獨具有本身的文學性，也是能使讀者在欣賞風景名勝獲取美感的同時，獲得語言上的教益。也出於這一目的，有些名著雖然屬知名度很高的上乘文學作品，也未能收入本書，如馬克‧吐溫蜚聲海內外的代表作《費恩歷險記》中的"大河日出"和"河上星空"等，都是意境很美的精品，但考慮到有方言和土語，也只好忍痛割愛。

由於文化背景上的差異和作品發表時代的不同，本書選段風格各異，題材內容多樣，呈現各家爭奇鬥艷的格局。譬如，麥爾維爾的作品以其出色的象徵和深遠的意境聞名於世，他那粗獷、雄渾的氣勢顯示了一種男性氣質的陽剛美。在《白鯨》裏有一段關於海洋的精彩描寫，是一個極好的例子：“在高空，這裏那裏，一些沒有斑點的小鳥，展開雪白的翅膀在滑翔；這就是女性氣質的天空，令人遐思翩翩；可是，在海裏，在海的無底深淵中，游弋着巨大的鯨、劍魚和鯊魚，這些是男性氣質的大海，它激起人們強烈的、惱人的、殺氣騰騰的思想”。

英國女作家夏洛蒂·勃朗特對自然景物的精緻、細膩的描繪，在“冬日小徑”、“賽似伊甸園”等篇幅有很好的展示。字裏行間充溢着女性氣息的秀麗，和麥爾維爾的風格形成對照。

法國作家福樓拜和羅蘭對大自然的精細入微、情趣盎然的描繪，分別在“仲秋圓月”和“甦醒的羅馬郊野”中可見一斑。他們的浪漫主義抒情和綺麗的文風顯然自成一派。

美國作家斯坦貝克，馬克·吐溫和女作家凱瑟跟上述法國作家完全相反，他們的作品格調清新，筆觸流暢，充滿濃厚的鄉土氣息，對大自然的觀察獨具慧眼，在“加州春色"、"日月交輝"、"太陽上的畫"和"風嘯雷鳴"中都有引人入勝的描繪。

名著翻譯,既苦又樂,苦,如同逆水行舟,每前進一步,都需付出艱辛努力;樂,如同觀光客,常為眼前的景色所陶醉,樂在其中。名著裏的精彩片段字字珠璣,給譯者一種無形的壓力感。優秀的譯文能給原作增姿添色,加強了名著的魅力;反之,一篇隨便的譯文有損名著的形象;譯者會有負疚感,是不能掉以輕心的。

譯者在翻譯過程中遇到的困難和問題,也大體相同。由於東西方在語言表達方式上的巨大差異,最讓人費神的恐怕是長句的翻譯問題。英語中長句多,結構複雜,要以流暢的中文表達長長的英文句子的含義,常令人左右為難。這一情況在較早出版的英美小說,如《無名的裘德》、《謝利》、《白鯨》等中尤為普遍。如在"古老的村莊"一段中就有這麼一句:"The site whereon so long had stood the ancient temple to the Christian divinities was not even recorded on the green and level grass-plot that had immemorially been the churchyard, the obliterated graves being commemorated by eighteen-penny cast-iron crosses warranted to last five years."這種長句即刻令人想起一棵根深葉茂、遮天蔽日的大樹來,由於枝椏過於繁茂,把整個主幹給湮沒了。只有當你弄清句子結構,才能真正明白它的意思,才能欣賞到這個古老的村莊的"廢墟之美"。

　　至於直譯與意譯的關係,事實上亦即形式與內容,或者"形似"與"神似"的關係。由於本書是英漢對照的讀物,更多需要的自然是比較接近英語原文的直譯,為此,翻譯時在遣詞造句方面,既要符合通順的漢語,又要不偏離原文的意義及結構。例如"荒涼的愛敦"中,最後一句話裏"appealed to"的譯法,就很有斟酌的地方。如將"appealed to"譯為"能夠令(荒涼的愛敦)感動的是……"就更為傳神。但由於本書是英漢對照的讀物,就不得不考慮另一種更為貼近原文的譯法:"能夠和荒涼的愛敦意氣相投的,是那種比較細膩和比較稀有的本性……"。但這種直譯在很多情況下還需有一定的靈活性。遇到難句,生硬的直譯常常是不能奏效的。一個較為典型的例子出自《白鯨》的"基多之春"結尾的一個句子:"Inward they turned upon the soul, especially when the still mild hours of eve came on; then, memory shot her crystals as the clear ice most forms of noiseless twilights"。這裏分號之後的子句"then, memory shot her crystals as the clear ice most forms of noiseless twilights"按照直譯,譯文為:"就像冰霜在萬籟俱寂的夜空裏結成冰晶體一樣,記憶也突然結晶了。"這譯文顯然詞不達意,讀者會問:"記憶是怎樣突然結晶的?"遇到這種情況,是需"靈活"的直譯了。

有時，一個詞的內涵可以反映出東西方不同文化背景和心理上的差異，在翻釋時就更需慎重對待。如出自馬克·吐溫的《鍍金時代》的選段"初升的太陽"裏有這麼一句："Venerable mudturtles crawled up and roosted upon the old logs in the stream..."這裏，"烏龜"的譯法就很有意思。在中國人的傳統心裏，烏龜似有一層模糊的貶義。但在西方國度裏並非如此。恰恰相反，在有些東西方國度裏，烏龜是長壽的象徵，許多人把它作為一種吉祥物對待。這樣"Venerable mudturtles"應譯為"古老可敬的烏龜"，而不是"令人厭惡的烏龜"。

　　誠然，限於譯者水平，也時會遇到一些意蘊特別深邃的原文，即使調動直譯與意譯的種種手段，仍覺不夠到位。這樣的例子在本書也定然不少。出自《白鯨》選段的"海天交融"中就有這麼一個例子，原文為："And at the girdling line of the horizon — denoted the fond, throbbing trust, the loving alarms, with which the poor bride gave her bosom away"。幾經琢磨，本書中的譯文為："而在腰帶似的地平綫上，有一陣多情的顫動——那個可憐的新娘，在獻出她的身心時那種迷戀、鍾情的激動。"但這個譯文依然給人某種欠缺之感。處理這類問題，就顯得相當棘手，也許要留待翻譯界以後去作認真的探討。

　　翻譯也是一項變化多端，千差萬別的工作，只有通過不斷的實踐，才能達到較為完美的境界。

PREFACE

The beauty of art is higher than nature

— Hegel: *Aesthetics*

Beauty is an ideal state, and a lofty pursuit of humankind. Nature amid which we live is full of mystery and wonder. Mountains and rivers, trees and flowers, mist and rain: every form of creation around us contains unique beauty which, augmented by the skilful description of poets and novelists, deeply impresses us. Admiration and enjoyment of the natural world is one of our original instincts. We go to Nature for relief and comfort in trouble, and harmony and accord in joy. A great part of our emotions, pleasurable or painful, stems from Nature. There is surely an inborn affinity between Nature and human beings. The appreciation of the beauty of Nature is, in truth, an accomplishment of civilization which we all learn as an art.

The description of natural scenery in great works of literature is a crystallization of natural beauty, artistic beauty as well as the beauty of the noble soul. It comes from Nature but transcends it. Scenic descriptions contribute to the literary works chiefly in the following ways:

I. For appreciation and enjoyment which relaxes the body and delights the soul

Nature, lavishes upon us her prodigious charm. Her majestic mountains, with girdling mist; her lush valleys, teeming with fertility; her boundless plains, with waves of verdure; her streams and rivers, rolling endlessly into the sea; her glossy lakes, rippling like quicksilver; her deep forests, putting forth all its luxuriant vegetation; her skies, adorned by ever-changing clouds and illuminated by magical moonlight and glorious sunshine — the sublime beauty of Nature manifests itself in every hour of the day, in every change of weather, and every change of season. All the year round there is scenery of various hues: spring is gay with flowers; summer is lush with deep green shades; autumn is bright with limpid skies; winter is decked with pure white snow. A savouring of the natural scenic beauty brings us the delight of relaxation and rest. Why not go ahead with it?

II. To build up a certain atmosphere in the story

It rarely appears that the depiction of nature in literary works exists for the sole reason of enjoyment. Scenic descriptions of nature, on many occasions, are loaded with meanings and allusions that serve to build up a certain atmosphere, or a certain mood in the story. By identifying the innermost feelings of the characters with the landscape descriptions, a writer brings the readers personally to the scene. A stroll through some gardens in blossom time in a quiet evening, as in "More Eden-like Nook", produces the leisurely and carefree mood. The falling yellow leaves on the path in "A Peaceful Autumn Day" declare the coming of late autumn, creating a sense of desolation. The beautiful scenery in "The Happy Valley", with light rain over the wooded hill and winding path, with flowers sending out sweet and heady scent and with the gentle murmur of the stream, offers us a mesmerizing landscape vignette. The fascinating richness of its view stimulates our aesthetic enjoyment. Watching the red sun sink in the western sky is certainly most exciting. It is one of those still moments for Mrs. Morel in *Sons and Lovers* as well as for every one of us. When such a moment comes, the small frets vanish, the beauty of things stands out, and we have the peace and the strength to see ourselves as Mrs. Morel does. The depiction of the scenery in "Camping" is magnificently conceived. It serves as an example of contrast: "...the silence and the beauty of this camp at night.... The stars! The mystic, shadowy water, faintly rippling in a light wind... the cries of night birds and owls..." arouses nothing but the inward distress of Clyde, the hero of the book. The mysteriously beautiful scenery around him contrasts with his brooding sadness and burning anxiety.

III. To provide the setting for the story

Many a description of natural scenery in literary works serves as the necessary stage for the activities of the characters. Among the selected passages included in this book, "The Dust" from *The Grapes of Wrath* by John Steinbeck, the Nobel Prize winner, is a good illustration. It clearly points out for the readers the geographical features of Oklahoma in Southeast America: the sun flaring down on the growing corn day by day, the surface of the earth crusted, the sky darkened by the mixing dust, the corn fighting the wind with its weakened leaves until the roots were freed by the prying wind... — a miserable picture of barren country.

"Haggard Egdon" from Hardy's *The Return of the Native* is a remarkable description of the natural scenery of Egdon Heath — the important background of the story. It came to be regarded as one of the exquisitely wrought pieces of prose work in English novels. Hardy describes Egdon Heath, which virtually embodies all the harshness and cruelties of nature, as "a spot which returned upon the memory of those who loved it with an aspect of peculiar and kindly congruity." "Twilight combined with the scenery of Egdon Heath to evolve a thing majestic without severity, impressive without showiness, emphatic in its admonitions, grand in its simplicity." This wonderful depiction of Egdon Heath not only provides a vivid setting for the tragic story but also adds beauty to the novel.

"The Delicious Vale" from Defoe's *Robinson Crusoe* draws for us a painting of the imaginary paradise on earth. But, instead of setting this in a certain secluded corner of the civilized world, we find it in a remote uninhabited island which is the very location of the story.

Selecting suitable material for this book is very much like choosing an ideal husband for a girl. A good deal of picking up and giving up was involved. It is not hard to imagine what great earnestness and expectation were attached to it. At all times and in all countries, great works of literature in the world's precious cultural heritage are innumerable. Opinions seem to differ as to which ones are considered great works of literature, and there is no authoritative list to consult. The present selections come largely from the works of those great masters deserved to be better known in the light of the booklist on the backcover of Cliffs Notes. Here is a partial list of these great works included in this selection: Hardy's *The Return of the Native, Tess of the d'Urbervilles, Mayor of Casterbridge*; Dickens' *David Copperfield, Oliver Twist, Great Expectations, The Old Curiosity Shop, The Bleak House*; Charlotte Brontë's *Jane Eyre*; Thackeray's *Vanity Fair*; D. H. Lawrence's *Sons and Lovers*; Melville's *Moby Dick*; Hawthorne's *The Scarlet Letter*; Henry James' *The Portrait of a Lady*; Lewis' *Main Street*; Hemingway's *The*

Sun Also Rises, A Farewell to Arms; Mark Twain's *The Adventures of Tom Sawyer*; Steinbeck's *the Grapes of Wrath*; Cather's *My Ántonia*; Leo Tolstoy's *War and Peace*; *Anna Karenina*; Sholokhov's *And Quiet Flows the Don*; Turgenev's *Fathers and Sons*; Rolland's *Jean Christophe*; Flaubert's *Madame Bovary*; Cervantes' *Don Quixote*. With a few exceptions, not more than three passages were taken from each book.

Language is a point for consideration, too, in the choice of the present material. Among the world's numerous great works, priority is given to English and American novels with a view to benefiting readers linguistically, since the best selection should be a piece which helps readers gain at once aesthetic delight and an understanding of the language. For this reason, some remarkable passages, e.g. the grand view of a sunrise on the Mississippi and the beauty and wonder of a sky all sparkling with stars from Mark Twain's representative work *The Adventures of Huckleberry Finn*, have reluctantly been given up for the presence of slang and dialectal language in it.

Owing to the difference in cultural backgrounds and the disparity of the publishing times between the great works, the selections in this book display a wide range of forms, styles and themes, with stylistic richness and diversity. For instance, Melville, whose writings are heavily symbolic and marked with classical allusions, possesses the beauty of masculine temperament. This is exemplified in *Moby Dick*, a work of unmatched brilliance. A strong element of fantasy and innovative imagery is vividly shown in the following wonderful depiction of the sea: "Hither, and thither, on high, glided the snow-white wings of small, unspeckled birds; these were the gentle thoughts of the feminine air; but to and fro in the deeps, far down in the bottomless blue, rushed mighty leviathans, sword-fish, and sharks; and these were the strong, troubled, murderous thinkings of the masculine sea."

In contrast, Charlotte Brontë's exuberance and exquisiteness in dealing with the scenic splendour of hills and rivers are well displayed in such selections as "The Winter Delight of a Lane" and "More Eden-like Nook". These passages show her art at its best and render the beauty of feminine delicacy to the full.

"The Perfectly Round Moon" and "The Awakening Campagna" contain superb descriptions of nature by Flaubert and Rolland respectively. They offer glimpses of the romantic lyricism and the ornate style of the great French writers.

Quite different from the above French writers, Steinbeck, Cather and Mark Twain all wrote in an original style marked by its freshness and poignancy. Their eyes were sensitive to the beauty of the wonders of nature as depicted in "Spring in California", "The Two Luminaries Confronted Each Other",

"A Picture Writing on the Sun", and "The Roaring Wind and the Booming Thunderblasts".

Translating great works of literature is a job both laborious and joyful: laborious because each step forward costs painstaking efforts, the process being like a boat sailing against the current; joyful because the translator is easily affected by the artistic appeal of the original work, like a tourist indulging himself or herself in the joy of appreciation. Each word of the present selection a gem. A good translation adds beauty to the original great work, which is a source of pressure for the translator, while a casual one would mar its image, which gives the translator a sense of guilt. We can never treat translation lightly.

By and large, I met the same problems and difficulties in the process of translating as other translators do. Owing to the great disparity of linguistic constructs between English and Chinese, one common problem is the rendering of a long complicated English sentence in Chinese. This frequently appears in the older English and American novels such as *Jude the Obscure*, *Shirley*, *Moby Dick*, etc. We have such an example in the selection "An Old-fashioned Little Village" which reads: "The site whereon so long had stood the ancient temple to the Christian divinities was not even recorded on the green and level grass plot that had immemorially been the churchyard, the obliterated graves being commemorated by eighteen-penny cast-iron crosses warranted to last five years." Such a long sentence gives one the image of a gigantic tree with darksome shade whose trunk lies hidden among its numerous branches with leaves. One could scarcely appreciate the beauty of the ruins described in the sentence without making clear its structure and meaning.

The relationship between literal and free translation is virtually a conflict between form and spirit, between likeness in letter or in spirit. As this book is a bilingual text, a Chinese translation closer to the English original is required. To answer this purpose, more heed is paid to wording and phrasing to achieve fluency in the target language in the light of the meaning and structure of the original. An example of this is the translation of the phrase "appealed to" in the passage " Haggard Egdon": "Haggard Egdon appealed to a subtler and scarcer instinct, to a more recently learnt emotion, than and fair." Here, "appealed to" is tentatively rendered into " 與……意氣相投的 ", though perhaps with less literary grace. Nevertheless this serves better the intention of the book. But this does not mean that a more literal translation is always needed. A certain flexibility is needed especially when we deal with a difficult sentence resulting either from its immensely difficult diction or from its profound implicit meaning. Here is an example from the passage "The Bright Quito Spring": "Inward they turn upon the soul, especially when the still mild hours of eve came on; then, memory shot her crystals as the clear ice most forms of noiseless twilights." A verbal translation of the "when-clause" in the sentence would read: "就像冰霜在萬籟俱寂的夜空裏結成冰的晶體一樣，記憶也突然結晶了。" Readers would reasonably ask: "How could memory shoot her crystals?" A puzzling question! A tentative translation is supplied in this selection.

Sometimes the implied meaning of a word may show up the great disparity of cultural background between the Eastern and the Western worlds. In such cases we need to be particularly careful in the translation. A sentence from the passage "The Sun Rose" reads: "Venerable mudturtles crawled up and roosted upon the old logs in the stream..." In the light of traditional Chinese culture, turtles seem to carry a vague derogative sense. But we find no bad connotation in turtles and the like in the Western tradition. Quite on the contrary, in some of the Western countries, and in some Asian countries too, the turtle is an emblem of longevity. So "venerable mudturtles" is rendered into "古老可敬的烏龜".

When dealing with some immensely difficult sentences, owing to the limitation of the translator, it is not easy to bring out a satisfying translaton to the readers — a version which possesses the likeness both in form and in spirit. Such instances are not rare in the present book. One example can be found in the passage, "The Firmaments of Air and Sea" from *Moby Dick*: "And at the girdling line of the horizon — denoted the fond, throbbing trust, the loving alarms, with which the poor bride gave her bosom away." After repeated attempts, a tentative version is provided: "而在腰帶似的地平綫上，有一陣多情的顫動——那個可憐的新娘在獻出她的身心時那種迷戀，鍾情的激動" Obviously, this version still leaves something to be desired. Problems like this are troublesome and we had better leave them for the translation circle to work out a more satisfactory version.

Translation is also an ever-changing task with thousands of results. A better translation can be attained only after constant trials and practices.

目 錄
CONTENTS

Day and Night　晝夜

xxviii

Landscapes 地貌

Other Scenery　其他景物

The Seasons
季節

1 The Real Spring Had Come

The spring had a slow start. During the last weeks of Lent[1] the weather had been clear and frosty. There was a thaw in the daylight sunshine, but at night the temperature sank to sixteen degrees Fahrenheit; the snow was crusted over so hard that carts did not have to stay on the roads. Easter took place under the snow. Then suddenly, on Easter Monday, a warm wind began blowing, clouds came up, and for three days and three nights a warm, stormy rain poured down. On Thursday the wind died down and a dense gray mist came up as though to hide the secrets of the changes that were taking place in nature. The melted snow rushed down beneath the mist, the river ice began cracking and moving forward, and the turbid, foaming torrents began flowing more rapidly; the following Monday, from evening on, the mist dissolved, the clouds broke up into fleecy[2] cloudlets, the sky cleared, and the real spring had come. In

---

1. Lent：大齋節，自聖靈降臨節起，至復活節前夕的四十個周日，為紀念耶穌在荒野禁食。

2. fleecy：羊毛一般柔軟潔白的；fleecy cloudlets：朵朵似羊毛般捲曲的小白雲。

一　春到人間

　　春天姍姍來遲，大齋節的最後幾星期天氣一直晴朗而
嚴寒，白天陽光可以融化冰雪，可是到夜晚，溫度就降到
了冰點以下七度。雪凍成這麼堅硬的一層冰殼，以致馬車
可以在沒有路的地方駛過。復活節來臨時滿地是雪，可
是，突然間，從復活節的第二天起颳起了溫暖的風，把雲
塊吹了過來，下了一場三天三夜和暖而猛烈的大雨。到星
期四，風停息了，大地上彌漫着灰色的濃霧，像是要把大
自然在變化中的秘密給掩蓋起來。融化了的雪水在霧下面
流動，河上的冰塊開始碎裂，向前漂浮。泛着泡沫，混濁
不清的急流更加快速地奔騰。復活節一周後的第一天，從
傍晚開始霧就散開了，雲簇化作朵朵捲曲的小白雲，天空
晴朗了，真正的春天來臨了。清晨，燦爛的太陽很快融解

the morning the bright sun quickly sucked up[3] the thin ice on the water, and the warm air all around throbbed with vapors from the awakening earth. The old grass grew green, as well as the young grass that pushed up in needle points; the buds swelled on the guelder-rose and the currant bush, and the birch trees were sticky with sap; honey bees began buzzing among the golden catkins of the willow. Unseen larks burst into song above the velvety green and the frozen stubble, peewits began crying above the lowlands and marshes where the water brought down by the storm was not yet absorbed; and cranes and geese flew high above giving their springtime call. The cattle, their winter coats still only gone in patches[4], began to low in the meadows, crook-legged lambs began frisking about their bleating mothers, just losing their wool; nimble-footed children began rushing about the quickly drying paths marked with the imprints of bare feet, the merry voices of women bleaching linen began chattering by the ponds, and the axes of the peasants getting their wooden plows and harrows ready began ringing out in the yards.

The real spring had come.

Lev Tolstoy: Anna Karenina

---

3. sucked up：原義“吸吮”，這裏形象地比喻太陽融解薄冰這一過程。

了水上的薄冰，溫暖的空氣因為從周圍甦醒了的大地上升起來的蒸汽而顫動了起來。隔年的草又開始發綠，新草長出了針尖般的葉片；繡球花和紅醋栗的芽苞顯得脹鼓鼓的，樺樹灌滿了樹汁，變得黏糊糊的，蜜蜂開始在柳樹枝上金色的柳絮中嗡嗡叫。看不見的雲雀在綠油油的田野和冰硬的殘茬上空引吭高歌，田鳧在雨後未乾的低窪地和沼澤上哀鳴，野鶴和野鵝展翅高飛，發出了春天的叫喊，牛羣身上的毛尚未完全脫落，就已經開始在草地上哞哞叫；彎腿小羔羊開始在他們咩咩叫着的母親們身旁活蹦亂跳又開始脫了毛；機靈的孩子們在印着腳印及迅速變乾的路面上來回奔跑着；池塘邊響起了洗衣農婦們愉快的閒談聲。院子裏聽得見農夫們製造木犂和耙的斧頭聲。

真正的春天來到了。

（俄）列夫·托爾斯泰：《安娜·卡列尼娜》

---

4. patches：原義 "補片"，這裏轉義形容牛身上脫了毛尚未完全脫淨的斑駁的形象。

2 Spring Was Coming into Its Own

Arkady was lost in these thoughts, while all around him spring was coming into its own[1]. Everything was turning a golden green, moving freely and shining softly under the gentle breath of the warm breeze, everything — the trees, the bushes, the grass. The larks deluged[2] it all with endless waves of song; the lapwings screeched from time to time, circling over low-lying meadows, then silently running over the hillocks; crows, looking handsomely black in the delicate verdure, became lost from sight walking through the low spring corn[3]; only their dark heads appeared from time to time in the smoky waves of the already whitening grain.

Ivan Turgenev: Fathers and Sons

---

1. coming into its own：進入繁榮期，盛行。
2. deluged：喻指聲音像洪水般湧來。
3. corn：英國指小麥。

二　春意濃

　　阿爾卡狄沉浸在這些思緒裏，不覺周圍一切春意正濃。到處一片金綠色，樹啊，矮林子啊，草啊，一切都在閃閃發光，並且在和煦的微風的輕拂下，輕柔地蕩漾着。雲雀陣陣嘹亮的歌聲不絕地淹過來；鳳頭麥雞時時發出尖叫聲，在低低的草地上盤旋，隨後靜靜地掠過小丘飛走了；烏鴉在低低的麥田裏走動着；在這一片葱綠的映襯下，一身烏黑的羽毛煞是美麗。牠們不一會兒就消失在已經變白了的裸麥中間，又不時從那煙霧一般的麥浪中探出頭來。

(俄) 屠格涅夫：《父與子》

3 The Great Spring Murmur

It was beautiful spring weather, but neither dogs nor humans were aware of it. Each day the sun rose earlier and set later. It was dawn by three in the morning, and twilight lingered till nine at night. The whole long day was a blaze of sunshine. The ghostly winter silence had given way to the great spring murmur of awakening life. The murmur arose from all the land, fraught with the joy of living. It came from the things that lived and moved again, things which had been as dead and which had not moved during the long months of frost. The sap was rising in the pines. The willows and aspens were bursting out in young buds. Shrubs and vines were putting on fresh garbs of green. Crickets sang in the nights, and in the days all manner of creeping, crawling things rustled forth into the sun. Partridges and woodpeckers were booming and knocking in the forest. Squirrels were chattering, birds singing, and overhead honked the wild-fowl driving up from the south in cunning wedges that split the air.

From every hill slope came the trickle of running water,

三　春之喧鬧

　　那是明媚的春天，可是，無論人或狗都沒有注意到。太陽一天比一天升得更早，落得更晚，早晨三點鐘就露出了黎明的曙光，黃昏卻一直要呆到夜晚九點鐘才告退。漫長的一天裏陽光璀璨，陰森可怕的冬之沉寂，已經讓位給春天裏復甦了的生命那壯觀的喧鬧。這種喧鬧發自大地各處，洋溢着生的喜悅。它來自那些生機盎然和重新活動着的東西，這些東西在漫長的冰凍時期曾經如同死去一般，一動都不動。松樹樹幹裏漲滿了樹汁，楊、柳都綻出了新芽，灌木叢和葛藤穿上了綠色新裝。夜晚蟋蟀在叫，白天各種各樣爬行的、蠕動的東西沙沙地爬進陽光裏。森林裏、鷓鴣在咕咕地叫；啄木鳥在篤篤地敲；松鼠在喊喊喳喳地叫；鳥兒在歡唱。頭頂上野雁在啼鳴，它們排成精巧的人字行從南方飛來，劃破長空。

　　潺潺的流水聲從每一座山坡上傳來，那是一條條看不

the music of unseen fountains. All things were thawing, bending, snapping. The Yukon[1] was straining to break loose the ice that bound it down. It ate away from beneath; the sun ate from above. Air-holes formed, fissures sprang and spread apart, while thin sections of ice fell through bodily into the river. And amid all this bursting, rending, throbbing of awakening life, under the blazing sun and through the soft-sighing breezes, like wayfarers to death, staggered the two men, the woman, and the huskies.

Jack London: <u>The Call of the Wild</u>

---

1. Yukon = Yukon River，育空河，北美洲大河。源出加拿大境內落磯山脈西側，西北流，到美國阿拉斯加境內折向西南流，注入白令海的諾頓灣。1897年，在育空河流域的克朗代克地區發現金礦，引起美國最後一代淘金熱潮。"淘金"，在很長時間內都是人們想像中實現"美國夢"的"捷徑"。

見的泉水奏出的音樂。萬物在解凍，在作動，在劈啪作響。育空河在奮力掙開束縛着它的冰雪，河水從下面侵蝕着，太陽從上面融化着。氣孔形成了，裂縫產生了，並且擴散開去，這時一塊塊薄冰碎裂，整個兒地掉進了河裏。而在甦醒的生命這一切爆發、碎裂和悸動之間，在燦爛的陽光下，兩個男人，一個女人，和幾隻赫斯基狗，穿過一陣陣輕輕嘆息的微風，像走向死亡的徒步旅行者那樣，在蹣跚地走着。

（美）傑克·倫敦：《荒野的呼喚》

4 Spring in California

The spring is beautiful in California. Valleys in which the fruit blossoms[1] are fragrant pink and white waters in a shallow sea[2]. Then the first tendrils of the grapes, swelling from the old gnarled vines, cascade down to cover the trunks. The full green hills are round and soft as breasts. And on the level vegetable lands are the mile-long rows of pale green lettuce and the spindly little cauliflowers, the grey-green unearthly artichoke plants.

And then the leaves break out on the trees, and the petals drop from the fruit trees and carpet the earth with pink and white. The centres of the blossoms swell and grow and colour: cherries and apples, peaches and pears, figs which close the flower in the fruit. All California quickens with produce, and the fruit grows heavy, and the limbs bend gradually under the fruit so that little crutches must be placed under them to support the weight.

John Steinbeck: The Grapes of Wrath

---

1. the fruit blossoms：這裏 fruit = fruit tree; blossoms：開花，這裏作
    動詞用。

四　加州春色

　　加利福尼亞的春天是美麗的。漫山遍野的果樹鮮花盛開，條條山谷宛如香氣撲鼻、紅白相間的淺海海水。多節的老葡萄藤長出了新的捲鬚，像瀑布似地披撒了下來，裹住了主幹。蒼翠的山頭渾圓而又柔軟，像女人的乳房一般。地面上的菜地裏，長着長達一整哩成行成行嫩綠色的萵苣，和形似紡錘的小花椰菜，還有綠裏帶白的神奇的薊菜。

　　隨後，樹上迅速綻出了樹葉，果樹落下花瓣，把地面鋪成了淡紅色和白色。花蕊越長越大，顏色也漸漸變深：有櫻桃和蘋果，桃子和梨子，還有把花包在果實裏的無花果。全加利福尼亞的農產品都在迅速地成熟起來，水果長得沉甸甸的，果實壓彎了枝條，底下必須支上小小的撐杆才行。

（美）斯坦倍克：《憤怒的葡萄》

2.　pink and white waters in a shallow sea：shallow sea 指 valleys; pink and white waters 指覆蓋在山谷上的一大片紅白花海。water 作複數時，意為大片的水，如海水、河水、湖水等。

5   The Green-flushed Steppe

The spring of 1919 was brilliant with unusual beauty. The April days were fine and as translucent as glass. Over the inaccessible, azure sweep[1] of heaven the flocks of wild geese and copper-tongued cranes floated, floated, overtaking the clouds, flying away to the north. On the pallid green pall[2] of the steppe[3] close to the ponds the swans that had come out to feed sparkled like scattered pearls. The birds sang and called continually in the water-meadows along the rivers. Over the flooded pools the geese called, preparing for flight, and the osiers[4] hissed incessantly with the amorous ecstasies of the drakes. The willows were green with catkins, the poplars blossomed with sticky, scented buds. The green-flushed steppe was drenched with inexpressible charm, flooded with the ancient scent of the bare black earth and the ever young grass.

Mikhail A. Sholokhov: And Quiet Flows the Don

---

1. sweep：範圍，視野。azure sweep of heaven：一片碧藍的天空。
2. pall：陰暗色的遮蓋物，比喻草原覆蓋的地方。

五 青葱的草原

　　1919年的春天閃爍出異乎尋常美麗的光輝，四月天都是些晴朗無雲的日子，天空像玻璃般透明。雁行和聽上去像銅喇叭叫聲的鶴羣，在高不可攀的蔚藍天空中飛呀，飛呀，牠們飛過了彩雲，一直往北而去。在靠近水池的淡綠色的大草原邊緣，有許多出來覓食的天鵝，牠們的羽毛閃閃發亮，像是撒落在地上的珍珠。沿河的水草邊，鳥兒們不停地鳴叫和喧噪，在水漲得滿滿的池塘裏，野鵝鳴叫着，準備要起飛。情意正濃的公鴨欣喜若狂，伴着柳樹不停的嘶嘶聲。柳樹發綠了，長出了芽苞，白楊樹上黏糊糊，香噴噴的花蕾也鼓了起來。綠油油的草原施展出難以描繪的魅力，洋溢着光禿的黑土的古老氣息和常新的嫩草味兒。

（俄）肖洛霍夫：《靜靜的頓河》

3.　steppe：僅有旱生植物的大草原。

4.　osiers：一種柳樹，尤指青剛柳，杞柳。

6　The Blue Sweep of the Don

From the south a warm, gracious wind was blowing, and white clouds were gathered in the west. Distant thunder rolled faintly, and the village was scented with the blessed, vital perfume of opening buds and the moist black earth. White-maned[1] waves coursed over the blue sweep[2] of the Don and here the wind was invigoratingly damp and bitter with the smell of rotting leaves and wet wood. The lower edge of the ploughed land, a velvety black patch along the slope of the hill, was steaming, and a haze was rising and beginning to drift over the Don-side hills. A skylark was singing with wild abandon right over the road, and marmots were whistling. And above this earth, which breathed with great fruitfulness and an abundance of life-giving strength, hung a proud and lofty sun.

Mikhail A Sholokhov: And Quiet Flows the Don

---

1. white-maned：原義"一頭白髮的"，這裏用以喻指波浪頂峯的白色浪頭。
2. sweep：不斷地流，浪的衝擊。這裏形象地表現出頓河的水面在春風的吹颺下不斷掀動的情景。

六　頓河春風

　　從南方吹來了一股溫暖、柔和的風，白雲在西邊天空積聚，遠處響起了隆隆的雷聲，村子裏飄蕩着綻開的花蕾和潮濕的黑土的芬芳氣味，洋溢着幸福和活力，頓河的藍色水面上湧動着一道道白色的浪頭。河面上漂着的腐葉和潮濕的木頭，使得這裏颳過的風帶着一種令人爽快的濕潤感和刺鼻味兒。山坡上，一塊犁過的地，柔軟烏黑；下端散發出一股股蒸汽，漫漫變成了升騰的霧靄，開始在頓河沿岸的山峯上飄蕩。雲雀在大路上空放聲歌唱，土撥鼠在吱吱地叫。在這塊充滿生機和豐饒的沃土之上，高懸着一個驕傲的太陽。

　　　　　　　　　　（俄）肖洛霍夫：《靜靜的頓河》

7　The Awakening Campagna

The budding spring entered into alliance with her[1]. The dream of new life was teeming[2] in the warmth of the slumbering air. The young green was wedding with the silver-gray of the olive-trees. Beneath the dark red arches of the ruined aqueducts[3] flowered the white almond-trees. In the awakening Campagna[4] waved the seas of grass and the triumphant flames of the poppies. Down the lawns of the villas flowed streams of purple anemones[5] and sheets of violets. The glycine[6] clambered up the umbrella-shaped pines, and the wind blowing over the city brought the scent of the roses of the Palatine[7].

Romain Rolland: Jean Christophe

---

1. her：這個 "her" 並非指某位女性，而是指前文提及的 "無處不在的光明"。這是一種擬人法的修辭手段（personification）。前文把光明比喻為人，有着 "笑容"，給大地帶來勃勃生機。
2. teeming：充滿，洋溢。這裏取其古意，表示 "生產"。
3. aqueduets：水道，渠道；指古羅馬的引水道。
4. Campagna：羅馬城四周的平原。

七 甦醒的羅馬郊野

　　欣欣向榮的春天伴隨着無處不在的光明，新生活的夢在昏昏欲睡的溫暖氣氛中萌芽。銀灰色的橄欖樹長了新綠，在毀壞了的水道暗紅色的圓拱下，杏樹開滿了白花。初醒的羅馬郊野春草起伏如綠波，罌粟花怒放紅似火，一行行紫色的海葵和成片成片的紫羅蘭像溪水般地在別墅的草坪上流動，藤蔓爬上了傘形的松樹，吹過城市的清風送來了帕拉蒂尼丘的玫瑰的幽香。

　　　　　　　　　　　　（法）羅曼·羅蘭：《約翰·克利斯朵夫》

---

5. anemones：銀蓮花屬植物，如白頭翁，秋牡丹，海葵。

6. glycine：原義糖膠，這裏轉義藤蔓，形容它如膠似漆，緊緊纏住松樹攀扶而上。

7. Palatine：帕拉蒂尼丘，古羅馬七丘之一，羅馬城即建於其上，＝the Palatine Hill。

8　Signs of the New Green

The land was flat — as flat as a table — with a waning growth of brown grass left over from the previous year, and stirring faintly in the morning breeze. Underneath were signs of the new green — the New Year's flag of its disposition.[1] For some reason a crystalline atmosphere enfolded the distant, hazy outlines of the city, holding the latter like a fly in amber and giving it an artistic subtlety which touched him.

Theodore Dreiser: <u>The Titan</u>

---

1. the New Year's flag of disposition：flag 原義 "旗幟"，這裏表示一種訊號、標誌；disposition 解 "性情"、"傾向"。整個片語指預示新的一年春天來臨的徵兆。

八　新綠

地是平坦的，——平坦得像桌面——地上長着去年殘留的黃褐色的野草，在晨風中微微地搖動。野草下面已有新綠——這是草木知春的徵兆。不知甚麼緣故，在這座城市遠遠的，朦朧的輪廓上面籠罩着一層透明的氣體，使城市像一隻埋進琥珀裏的蒼蠅，賦與這座城市一種微妙的藝術感，這讓他感動了。

(美) 德萊塞：《巨人》

9 Flashing Country

One week of authentic[1] spring, one rare sweet week of May, one tranquil moment between the blast of winter and the charge of summer. Daily Carol walked from town into flashing country hysteric with new life.

One enchanted hour when she returned to youth and a belief in the possibility of beauty.

...

The thick grass beside the track, coarse and prickly[2] with many burnings[3], hid canary-yellow buttercups and the mauve petals and woolly sage-green coats of the pasque flowers. The branches of the kinnikinic[4] brush were red and smooth as lacquer on a saki[5] bowl.

She ran down the gravelly embankment, smiled at children gathering flowers in a little basket, thrust a handful of the soft pasque flowers into the bosom of her white blouse.

---

1. authentic：真正的；authentic spring 譯作 "仲春"，是因為仲春是春季的第二個月，既非 "初春"，也非 "暮春"，是 "真正的春天"。
2. prickly：刺痛的。

九　繁花似錦的鄉野

時值五月仲春時節，在一個難得的溫煦宜人的星期，一個在凜冽的隆冬和難熬的酷暑之間的安寧瞬間，每天卡羅爾都要從鎮上走向繁花似錦，生機勃勃的鄉野。

那是一個醉人的時刻，她彷彿覺得自己又回到了青年時代，深信世上確實有美的事物。

……

鐵路兩旁，荒草叢生，雜亂不堪，多次燒荒後剩下的殘莖枯茬還會扎人。草叢裏露出了鮮黃色的金風花，還有紫紅色的花瓣和毛茸茸的灰綠色的白頭翁。有一叢小灌木，它的枝葉紅嫣嫣，光溜溜的，看上去像塗在日本米酒杯上的釉彩。

她順着礫石堤岸跑過去，向提着小藍子採摘鮮花的孩子們頻頻微笑，把一束柔美的白頭翁插進她那潔白罩衫胸

---

3. burnings：指在野地燒荒草。

4. kinnikinic：一種石南科小灌木；山茱萸。

5. saki：日本米酒

Fields of springing wheat drew her from the straight propriety of the railroad and she crawled through the rusty barbed-wire fence. She followed a furrow between low wheat blades and a field of rye which showed silver lights as it flowed before the wind. She found a pasture by the lake. So sprinkled was the pasture with rag-baby blossoms and the cottony herb of Indian tobacco that it spread out like a rare old Persian carpet of cream and rose and delicate green. Under her feet the rough grass made a pleasant crunching. Sweet winds blew from the sunny lake beside her, and small waves sputtered on the meadowy shore. She leaped a tiny creek bowered[6] in pussy-willow buds. She was nearing a frivolous[7] grove of birch and poplar and wild plum trees.

The poplar foliage had the downiness of a Corot[8] arbor[9], the green and silver trunks were as candid as the birches, as slender and lustrous as the limbs of a Pierrot[10]. The cloudy white blossoms of the plum trees filled the grove with a springtime mistiness which gave an illusion of distance.

---

6. bowered in：bower 為由植物枝葉搭成的遮陰棚或涼亭。這裏指 "覆蓋着"。

7. frivolous：原義 "瑣碎的"，這裏指雜亂的。

前的衣袋裏。塊塊綠油油的麥田誘使她離開了筆直的鐵路綫，爬過了鏽迹斑斑的鐵絲網。她沿着低矮的小麥草和裸麥田之間的犂溝往前走，微風吹過，裸麥田裏銀光閃閃。她在湖畔發現了一塊草地，草地上開滿了五顏六色的野花，和印第安煙草雪白的絨花。一眼望去，像是一塊稀有的古代波斯地毯，上面奶油色、玫瑰色、淺綠色相映成趣。野棘在她的腳底下嘎吱嘎吱作響。陽光燦爛的湖面上，和風輕拂。芳草如茵的湖岸浪花飛濺。她縱身一躍，跳過了一條落滿柳絮的小溪，來到了一片熱鬧的小樹林跟前。那裏長滿了白樺樹、白楊樹和野李子樹。

白楊樹上的葉子，如同葛魯畫的樹一般，都有一層絨毛；綠色和銀白色的樹幹，像白樺樹那樣直溜溜的。又像小丑的四肢細長而富有光澤。野梨樹上繁花點點，一片白花花的，彷彿朦朧的春霧，逶迤飄渺。

---

8. Corot：葛魯，十九世紀風景畫家。
9. arbor：植物學用語，樹；喬木。也可解作遮陰棚，＝ bower。
10. Pierrot：法國啞劇中的丑角。

She ran into the wood, crying out for joy of freedom regained after winter. Choke-cherry blossoms lured her from the outer sun-warmed spaces to depths of green stillness, where a submarine light came through the young leaves. She walked pensively along an abandoned road. She found a moccasin-flower beside a lichen-covered log. At the end of the road she saw the open acres — dipping rolling fields bright with wheat.

...

She came out on the prairie, spacious under an arch[11] of boldly cut clouds. Small pools glittered. Above a marsh red-winged blackbirds chased a crow in a swift melodrama of the air. On a hill was silhouetted a man following a drag. His horse bent its neck and plodded, content.

A path took her to the Corinth road, leading back to town. Dandelions glowed in patches amidst the wild grass by the way. A stream galloped through a concrete culvert beneath the road.

Sinclair Lewis: Main Street

---

11. arch：原義 "拱門"，這裏指天空。

她跑進樹林裏，為冬天過去，重獲自由而大聲歡呼。野櫻桃樹上繁花似錦，使她情不自禁地離開了林外暖洋洋的空地，信步走進了寂靜的綠蔭叢中。那裏，陽光透過嫩葉，投下幽幽的光。她若有所思地沿着一條荒蕪的小道往前走，在一根長滿地衣的圓木旁邊，她意外地發現了一朵枸蘭。小路盡頭，她看到了一望無際的田野—— 一片麥浪起伏的農田。

……

她走出了小樹林，來到了大草原。天空佈滿了詭譎奇特的雲層，蒼穹底下大草原顯得格外寬廣。小池塘在閃閃發光，沼澤地上空，一羣紅翅膀的黑乙鳥正追逐着一隻烏鴉，在空中瞬即掀起一場鬧劇。小山坡上，映出一個男人扶着犁杖耕地的剪影，他的馬正埋着頭奮力往前拉，蠻滿意的。

她沿着一條小徑走上了回到小鎮的大路。一簇簇的蒲公英在路旁雜草叢中，顯得分外艷麗奪目。大路底下，一條小溪正在水泥下水道裏奔流。

（美）辛克萊·路易斯：《大街》

10　The Bright Quito Spring

Some days elapsed, and ice and icebergs all astern[1], the Pequod now went rolling through the bright Quito[2] spring, which, at sea, almost perpetually reigns on the threshold of the eternal August of the Tropic. The warmly cool[3], clear, ringing, perfumed, overflowing, redundant days, were as crystal goblets of Persian sherbet[4], heaped up — flaked up, with rose-water snow. The starred and stately nights seemed haughty dames in jewelled velvets, nursing at home in lonely pride, the memory of their absent conquering Earls, the golden helmeted suns[5]! For sleeping man, 'twas[6] hard to choose between such winsome days and such seducing nights. But all the witcheries of that unwaning weather did not merely lend new spells and potencies to the outward world. Inward they turned upon the soul, especially when the still mild hours

---

1. astern：在船尾，這裏指在後面。
2. Quito：基多，南美厄瓜多爾的首都。位於赤道以南皮欽查山東麓的谷地中。氣候溫和，年均氣溫13℃ —14℃。
3. warmly cool：令人愉悦的涼爽；又溫和，又涼爽，這是一個矛盾修辭法(oxymoron)的例子。

28

十　基多之春

　　過了些日子，冰塊和冰山全都給拋到了後面，這時，"裴各德號"乘風破浪，駛進了春光明媚的基多，在海洋上的基多，春天幾乎總是徜徉在熱帶永恆的八月的門口，碧空萬里，涼爽宜人，鳥語花香。豐溢漫長的白晝，如同波斯那種盛冰果子露的水晶杯子，堆滿了用玫瑰香水製成的冰片。繁星閃爍，端莊肅穆的夜空，宛如一些身穿天鵝絨衣服，滿身珠光寶氣的傲慢的貴婦，高傲孤單地待在家裏，默默想念着不在她們身邊的南征北戰的公侯，想念她們那些盔甲輝煌的太陽。對貪睡的人而言，這種迷人的白晝和誘人的夜晚一樣，都可以酣睡。不過，這種像魔法般的燦爛天氣，不光是給外界增添了新的魅力，還打開了人

4.　sherbet：英國為果子露，美國指果汁與牛奶等製成的冰糕。

5.　suns：此處語帶雙關，指黑夜的夫婿，那些公侯，像她們的太陽一樣。亦可指榮耀。

6.　'twas = it was

of eve came on; then, memory shot her crystals as the clear
ice most forms of noiseless twilights[7].

Herman Melville: Moby Dick

---

7. 最後一句話 "Inward …" 中的 they 指前句的 that unwaning
   weather，這整句話的內涵深邃而晦澀，第一分句渲染這種燦爛天
   氣對人們心靈的魅力；第二分句強調這種魅力作用的結果。這裏
   memory 指人們對往事的回憶，crystal 在此解為水晶般清澈透明的東
   西。

們的心扉，尤其是在靜謐柔美的夜色降臨的時刻；如同晶瑩的冰塊大都是在萬籟俱寂的夜空裏凝結而成，此刻人們對往事的回憶也突然變得清晰無比。

(美) 麥爾維爾：《白鯨》

11　The Prime and Vigour of the Year

Spring flew swiftly by, and summer came. If the village had been beautiful at first it was now in the full glow and luxuriance of its richness. The great trees, which had looked shrunken and bare in the earlier months, had now burst into strong life and health; and stretching forth their green arms over the thirsty ground, converted open and naked spots into choice nooks, where was a deep and pleasant shade from which to look upon the wide prospect, steeped in sunshine, which lay stretched beyond. The earth had donned her mantle of brightest green; and shed her richest perfumes abroad. It was the prime and vigour of the year; all things were glad and flourishing.

Charles Dickens: Oliver Twist

十一 盛夏的活力

　　春天已飄然而去，夏天來了。如果說春天的鄉村景色
旖旎，那麼，夏天的鄉村正展示出它全部的魅力和豐盈。
那些早幾個月還顯得枯瘦、光禿的大樹，如今生氣勃勃，
精力充沛。它們伸出了碧油油的臂膀，遮蓋着焦渴的地
面，把裸露的空地變成濃蔭遮蔽、幽靜宜人的去處，從那
裏可以眺望沐浴在陽光下，一直伸展開去的廣闊天地。大
地披上了青翠欲滴的盛裝，散發出濃郁醉人的芬芳。現在
正值一年的黃金時期，萬物欣欣向榮，一派歡樂景象。

　　　　　　　　　　　　　(英)　狄更斯：《苦海孤雛》

12　A Splendid Midsummer

A splendid midsummer shone over England: skies so pure, suns so radiant as were then seen in long succession, seldom favour, even singly, our wave-girt land[1]. It was as if a band of Italian days had come from the South, like a flock of glorious passenger birds, and lighted to rest them on the cliffs of Albion[2]. The hay was all got in; the fields round Thornfield were green and shorn; the roads white and baked; the trees were in their dark prime; hedge and wood, full-leaved and deeply tinted, contrasted well with the sunny hue of the cleared meadows between.

Charlotte Brontë: Jane Eyre

1.　our wave-girt land：喻指英格蘭。
2.　Albion：阿爾比恩，英格蘭或不列顛的舊稱。

十二 英格蘭仲夏

　　明媚的仲夏照耀着英格蘭：天空如此明淨，太陽這般燦爛，在我們這塊波濤圍繞的地方，這樣美好的天氣哪怕是一天也難得降臨。而現在卻接連許多天都這樣，彷彿一連串的意大利天氣，像一羣歡快的過路鳥，棲息在阿爾比恩的懸崖上。乾草已經全都收起來了；桑菲爾德周圍的田野一片葱蘢，像修剪過一樣；道路讓太陽曬得刷白，烘得乾乾的；樹木鬱鬱葱葱；樹籬和樹林枝葉茂盛，色澤濃綠，和它們之間滿地陽光明朗的牧草地形成了很好的對比。

（英）夏洛蒂・勃朗特：《簡・愛》

13 Thermidor

July passed over their heads, and the Thermidorean[1] weather which came in its wake[2] seemed an effort on the part of Nature to match the state of hearts at Talbothays Dairy. The air of the place, so fresh in the spring and early summer, was stagnant and enervating now. Its heavy scents weighed upon them, and at mid-day the landscape seemed lying in a swoon. Ethiopic[3] scorchings browned the upper slopes of the pastures, but there was still bright green herbage here where the watercourses purled. And as Clare was oppressed by the outward heats, so was he burdened inwardly by waxing fervour of passion for the soft and silent Tess.

Thomas Hardy: Tess of the d'Urbervilles

---

1. Thermidorean：歷史用語，熱月的。該詞來源於 Thermidor 熱月，亦即法國資產階級革命時期共和曆的第十一月，相當於公曆七月十九日到八月十七日。資產階級右翼集團在熱月發動政變，推翻雅各賓（Jacobin）專政，建立熱月黨反動統治。
2. in its wake：隨着⋯⋯之後。
3. Ethiopic：衣索比亞的。Ethiopia 為非洲國家，原稱 Abyssinia（阿比西尼亞）。

十三　暑月

七月過去了，接着到來的是"暑月"。這彷彿是大自然這方有意作出的努力，使它和塔布西牛奶廠上情人的心情相呼應。這個地方的空氣，在春天和初夏的時候原本非常清新，現在卻變得呆滯和柔弱無力。濃郁的氣息老壓在他們上面，正午的時候，整個大地好像都昏昏睡去。牧場上較高的山坡，都被如同衣索比亞一般灼熱的陽光烤成褐色。不過，在這裏水聲淙淙的溝渠邊，也還有青翠的草色。克萊爾在受暑熱蒸烤的同時，對溫婉嫻雅的苔絲的熾烈感情，也使他的內心遭受着煎熬。

(英) 哈代：《德伯家的苔絲》

14 A Hot Summer Day

The streets were hot and dusty on the summer day, and the sun was so bright that it even shone through the heavy vapour drooping over Coketown, and could not be looked at steadily. Stokers emerged from low underground doorways into factory yards, and sat on steps, and posts, and palings, wiping their swarthy visages, and contemplating coals. The whole town seemed to be frying in oil. There was a stifling smell of hot oil everywhere. The steam-engines shone with it, the dresses of the Hands[1] were soiled with it, the mills throughout their many stories oozed and trickled it. The atmosphere of those Fairy Palaces was like the breath of the simoom[2], and their inhabitants, wasting with heat, toiled languidly in the desert. But no temperature made the melancholy mad elephants more mad or more sane. Their wearisome heads went up and down at the same rate, in hot weather and cold, wet weather and dry, fair weather and foul.

Charles Dickens: Hard Times

---

1. Hands：這裏轉義 "僱工"，"勞力"。
2. simoom：（氣象用語）西蒙風（阿拉伯、敘利亞、非洲等地的乾熱風）。

十四　炎炎夏日

夏日裏，那些街道灰塵撲面，酷勢難當。陽光甚至透過籠罩在焦炭鎮上空的一層厚厚的煙霧，強烈地照射下來，使人不敢正目而視。火夫們從低矮的地下室出來，走進工廠的場院裏，坐在台階上，柱子上和柵欄上，擦着他們黝黑的臉，盯着看煤堆。整個市鎮都像是在沸油鍋裏煎熬着，到處都散發着讓人窒息的熟油味兒。蒸汽機發着油光，工人的衣服上也都沾上了油污，工廠裏的許多樓層都在滲着油，滴着油。那些童話中的宮殿裏的氣氛就像陣陣熱風一般，在酷暑的折磨下，那兒的居民們消瘦了，無精打采地在沙漠中勞動着。可是，不論何種溫度都不會使得那些憂鬱得發狂的大象變得更為瘋狂，或者更為清醒，它們那令人生厭的腦袋不論天氣是熱是冷，是潮濕或是乾燥，是好天氣還是壞天氣，總是以同樣的頻率上下擺動着。

（英）狄更斯：《艱難時世》

15 Autumn Had Begun

In plain commonplace matter of fact, then, it was a fine morning — so fine that you would scarcely have believed that the few months of an English summer had yet flown by. Hedges, fields, and trees, hill and moorland, presented to the eye their ever-varying shades of deep rich green; scarce[1] a leaf had fallen; scarce a sprinkle of yellow mingled with the hues of summer warned you that autumn had begun. The sky was cloudless; the sun shone out bright and warm; the songs of birds and hum of myriads of summer insects filled the air; and the cottage gardens, crowded with flowers of every rich and beautiful tint, sparkled in the heavy dew-like beds of glittering jewels. Everything bore the stamp of summer, and none of its beautiful colours had yet faded from the dye.

Charles Dickens: The Pickwick Papers

---

1. scarce（古舊用法）= scarcely

十五　秋來夏未去

　　用最最普通的話來說，這是一個天氣晴朗的早晨——
如此晴朗，你幾乎都不能相信英格蘭那沒幾個月的夏季已
經飛逝。樹籬、田野、樹木、山巒和原野，在眼前呈現出
始終變換着的濃綠色調；幾乎見不到一片落葉；在夏季的
色澤中，幾乎見不到些微黃色，提醒你秋天已經開始。天
空明淨無雲；陽光燦爛而溫暖；空中洋溢着小鳥的歌聲，
和無數的夏季昆蟲的低鳴聲；村舍邊的小花園裏開滿了五
顏六色的鮮花，在華濃的露水中閃爍着，像是鋪滿了燦爛
珠寶的花牀。萬物都帶着夏季的特徵，夏天的美麗顏色還
一點也沒有消褪。

　　　　　　　　　　（英）狄更斯：《匹克威克外傳》

16 August

There is no month in the whole year in which nature wears a more beautiful appearance than in the month of August. Spring has many beauties, and May is a fresh and blooming month, but the charms of this time of year are enhanced by their contrast with the winter season. August has no such advantage. It comes when we remember nothing but clear skies, green fields, and sweet-smelling flowers — when the recollection of snow and ice and bleak winds has faded from our minds as completely as they have disappeared from the earth — and yet what a pleasant time it is! Orchards and cornfields ring with the hum of labour; trees bend beneath the thick clusters of rich fruit, which bow their branches to the ground; and the corn, piled in graceful sheaves or waving in every light breath that sweeps above it, as if it wooed the sickle[1], tinges the landscape with a golden hue. A mellow[2] softness appears to hang over the whole earth; the influence of the season seems to extend itself to the very waggon, whose

---

1. wooed the sickle：woo 原義為"求愛"、"求結合"，這裏意為在鐮刀面前弄姿作態，以博取青睞。
2. mellow：原義為"醇美"，常跟秋天果子成熟連用作比喻。

42

十六　八月

　　一年十二個月中，大自然的外貌最美不過的是八月。春天美不勝收，五月是百花盛開的嬌艷月份，但是，這一時節的魅力是由於和冬季的相比而得到加強的。八月沒有這種有利條件，它到來的時候我們只記得晴朗的天空，綠色的田野和芬芳的鮮花——冰、雪和凜冽的寒風已經完全從我們的腦海中消失，猶如它們已經完全從地球上消失一般。然而，八月是多麼令人愉快的時節啊！果園和田野響起了勞動者低吟的歌聲，樹上結滿了累累碩果，把枝條壓得彎彎的，低低地垂到地面上；而穀物呢，不是整整齊齊地堆疊着，便是被掠過的微風吹得搖搖晃晃，像是在向鐮刀獻媚，它們給這片風景染上一片金黃色。整個大地洋溢着豐收祥和的氣氛；這種季節的氣氛似乎也感染了馬車，

slow motion across the well-reaped field is perceptible only to the eye, but strikes with no harsh sound upon the ear.

Charles Dickens: <u>Pickwick Papers</u>

只有眼睛能夠看見它在收割乾淨的田野上緩緩移動，而耳朵卻聽不見它的粗濁的嗓音。

（英）狄更斯：《匹克威克外傳》

17 A Peaceful Autumn Day

It was a peaceful autumn day. The gilding of the Indian summer[1] mellowed the pastures far and wide. The russet woods stood ripe to be stript, but were yet full of leaf. The purple of heath-bloom, faded but not withered, tinged the hills. The beck wandered down to the Hollow, through a silent district; no wind followed its course, or haunted its woody borders. Fieldhead gardens bore the seal of[2] gentle decay. On the walks, swept that morning, yellow leaves had fluttered down again. Its time of flowers, and even of fruits, was over; but a scantling of apples enriched the trees; only a blossom here and there expanded pale and delicate amidst a knot of faded leaves.

Charlotte Brontë: Shirley

---

1. Indian summer：小陽春，指秋冬之間的一段溫暖的日子。
2. bear the seal of：原義"帶着印記"，這裏表示顯露出迹象。

十七 寧靜的秋日

　　這是個寧靜的秋日，小陽春的光彩把遼闊的牧場塗上一片金秋色彩。黃褐色的樹木雖已熟得可以折枝剝皮，卻仍然枝繁葉茂。紫紅色的石楠花雖已退色，但還未凋謝，把山崗點綴得斑斑駁駁。山溪淌過一段寂靜的地方，蜿蜒流至窪地；風兒沒有追逐着流水吹去，也沒有出沒於樹林的邊緣。菲爾哈德莊園已呈現出凋零之態，那天早晨，在那些剛剛清掃過的小徑上，黃葉又颼颼地飄落一地。莊園的百花盛開，果實累累的時節都已經過去。可是，還有少量蘋果在為樹木增姿添色；這裏那裏，還有一、二朵暗淡而柔弱的小花夾雜在一簇枯萎的黃葉之中。

　　　　　　　　　　（英）夏洛蒂·勃朗特：《謝利》

18　A California Indian Summer Day

Came a beautiful fall day, warm and languid, palpitant[1] with the hush of the changing season, a California Indian summer day, with hazy sun and wandering wisps of breeze that did not stir the slumber of the air. Filmy purple mists, that were not vapors but fabrics woven of color, hid in the recesses of the hills. San Francisco lay like a blur of smoke upon her heights. The intervening bay was a dull sheen of molten metal, whereon sailing craft lay motionless or drifted with the lazy tide. Far Tamalpais[2], barely seen in the silver haze, bulked hugely by the Golden Gate[3], the latter a pale gold pathway under the westering sun. Beyond, the Pacific, dim and vast, was raising on its skyline tumbled cloud-masses that swept landward, giving warning of the first blustering[4] breath of winter.

Jack London: Martin Eden

---

1. palpitant：悸動的、震盪着的；這裏有 "充滿着" 的意思。
2. Tamalpais：塔馬爾派斯山，位於舊金山西北，從山頂俯瞰，一面是太平洋，一面是舊金山灣，風景旖旎。

十八　加州小陽春

　　一個美麗的秋日來臨了，那是個加利福尼亞小陽春的日子，溫和而睏人，盪漾着季節更迭的寂靜。太陽曚曚曨曨，微風徐徐吹動，但並不驚擾這昏昏欲睡的氣氛。薄薄的紫色霧靄不是水氣，而是色彩交織成的帷幕，隱藏在羣山的深處。舊金山像一團模糊的輕煙，躺在山崗之巔。羣山環抱的海灣像熔化了的金屬，發出暗淡的光澤。水面上點點帆船，有的紋絲不動地躺着，有的隨着緩緩的水流漂動。遠處的塔馬爾派斯山，在銀色的霧靄中隱約可辨，巍然聳立在金門海峽一旁。這海峽在西斜的陽光中，宛如一條淡金色的通道。再遠處，便是隱隱約約，茫然一片的太平洋，在天際湧起一堆堆滾滾的雲塊。它們正朝着陸地洶湧而來，警告人們冬季第一股狂風即將來臨。

　　　　　　　　　　　　（美）傑克‧倫敦《馬丁‧伊登》

---

3. Golden Gate：金門海峽，位於舊金山北面，是舊金山通太平洋的一條狹長海峽。

4. blustering：（風）狂吹，咆哮。

19   The Long, Keen Breaths of Winter

Once the bright days of summer pass by, a city takes on
that sombre garb of grey, wrapt in which it goes about its
labours[1] during the long winter. Its endless buildings look
grey, its sky and its streets assume a sombre hue; the scattered,
leafless trees and wind-blown dust and paper but add to the
general solemnity of colour. There seems to be something in
the chill breezes which scurry through the long, narrow
thoroughfares productive of rueful thoughts. Not poets alone,
nor artists, nor that superior order of mind which arrogates
to itself all refinement, feel this, but dogs and all men. These
feel as much as the poet, though they have not the same power
of expression. The sparrow upon the wire, the cat in the
doorway, the dray horse[2] tugging his weary load, feel the
long, keen breaths of winter. It strikes to the heart of all life,
animate and inanimate[3]. If it were not for the artificial fires[4]
of merriment, the rush of profit-seeking trade, and pleasure-

---

1. labours：勞動；這裏為苦苦掙扎，努力挨過之意。
2. dray horse：運貨馬車的馬。
3. animate and inanimate：動物與非動物。
4. fires：激情、狂熱。

十九　嚴冬氣息

夏天晴朗的日子一旦過去，城市就披上了陰沉沉的灰色外衣，一副準備挨過漫長的冬天的打扮。無邊無際的房屋望去灰濛濛的，天空和街道也都染上了陰暗的色彩；一些落了葉子的枯樹禿枝，隨風飄蕩的塵埃和廢紙，都增添了這種蕭穆的情調。冷風疾速掠過又長又窄的大街，彷彿給人們帶來了某種哀思。不僅僅是詩人，也不僅僅是藝術家，或者那些自命不凡的文人雅士們感覺到了，連狗和普通人也都有同感。儘管他們沒有詩人那樣的表達能力，他們和詩人都有同樣的感受。電綫上的麻雀，門口的貓，負重的瘦馬，都感覺到了漫長嚴冬的氣息。冬天觸動了一切有靈性的，無靈性的生命體的心靈。若不是刻意追求歡樂的激情，孜孜為利的商業活動和給人以消遣的娛樂；若不

selling amusements; if the various merchants failed to make the customary display within and without their establishments; if our streets were not strung with signs of gorgeous hues and thronged with hurrying purchasers, we would quickly discover how firmly the chill hand of winter lays upon the heart; how dispiriting are the days during which the sun withholds a portion of our allowance of light and warmth. We are more dependent upon these things than is often thought. We are insects produced by heat, and pass without it[5].

Theodore Dreiser: <u>Sister Carrie</u>

---

5. 德萊塞是美國早期的自然主義者，自然主義思潮在他一些早期小說，尤其是《嘉莉妹妹》中時有流露。他深信人是環境和天性本能的犧牲品，其命運是不由自主的。這一選段的結尾也流露了這一思想。

是商店內外形形色色招徠顧客的展示和陳設；若我們的大街不是掛滿了五顏六色的招牌，擠滿了川流不息的顧客，我們會很快覺察到，這隻嚴冬的手是多麼沉重地壓在我們的心頭。太陽吝嗇地收回給人的一點光和熱，這樣的日子又是讓人多麼沮喪！我們對這些東西的依靠遠過於我們平日所想像的。我們是熱量產生的蟲豸，沒有熱量就不能生存。

（美）德萊塞：《嘉莉妹妹》

20　A North Pole Colouring

At length the latter autumn passed: its fogs, its rains withdrew from England their mourning and their tears[1]; its winds swept on to sigh over lands far away. Behind November came deep winter; clearness, stillness, frost accompanying.

A calm day had settled into a crystalline evening; the world wore a North Pole colouring: all its lights and tints looked like the 'reflets'[2] of white, or violet, or pale green gems. The hills wore a lilac-blue; the setting sun had purple in its red; the sky was ice, all silvered azure; when the stars rose, they were of white crystal — not gold; gray, or cerulean, or faint emerald hues — cool, pure, and transparent — tinged the mass of the landscape.

Charlotte Brontë: Shirley

1.　their mourning and their tears：整句中的 fogs 和 rains 本身是鮮明的形象，而 their mourning and their tears 又構成巧妙的比喻。大霧和細雨是英格蘭常見而又頗具特色的景象；但同時也給人們生活帶來諸多不便，因而被比喻成"服喪"和"流淚"，表達了一種令人生厭，想盡快擺脫之情。

二十　一抹北極色調

晚秋終於消逝；晚秋的霧，晚秋的雨，全都在英格蘭脫掉了喪服，抹去了淚水；寒風陣陣掠過，不斷向着遠方呼嘯而去，十一月之後隆冬接踵而至，隨之而來的是晴朗、寂靜、和嚴寒霜凍。

白天寧靜無風，黃昏天空一片清澄；世界一抹北極色調：所有的光和色，都像是種白色的"折光"，或紫色的，淡綠色的寶石光。山巒披上了紫丁香藍色；夕陽紅裏透紫；天空宛如薄冰；一片銀光閃閃的蔚藍色，星星露面時都不是金光燦爛，而是雪白的水晶體。整片景色都抹上了一層灰色，天青色，或者淡淡的翡翠色——清涼、純淨而透明。

（英）夏洛蒂·勃朗特：《謝利》

---

2. reflets：原文為法語"reflets"，作者作了如下腳註："讀者請為
　　我找個類似的英語詞，我將樂於不用這個法語詞彙。英語的
　　'reflections'不管用"。

21　The Winter Delight of a Lane

The ground was hard, the air was still, my road was lonely: I walked fast till I got warm, and then I walked slowly to enjoy and to analyse the species of pleasure brooding for me in the hour and situation. It was three o'clock; the churchbell tolled as I passed under the belfry: the charm of the hour lay in its approaching dimness, in the low-gliding and pale-beaming sun. I was a mile from Thornfield, in a lane noted for wild roses in summer, for nuts and blackberries in autumn, and even now possessing a few coral treasures[1] in hips and haws, but whose best winter delight lay in its utter solitude and leafless repose. If a breath of air stirred, it made no sound here; for there was not a holly, not an evergreen to rustle, and the stripped hawthorn and hazel bushes were as still as the white worn stones which causewayed the middle of the path. Far and wide, on each side,

---

1.　coral treasures：這裏比喻稀少之物。在寒冬臘月光禿禿的樹枝上，依然掛着幾顆薔薇，山楂之類的果實，這無異於"珍果"了。此外，珊瑚顏色繽紛（多呈粉紅色），更為嚴冬抹上色彩。

二十一　冬日小徑

　　路面堅實，空氣寧靜，我的旅途是孤寂的。我走得很
快，直到我覺得暖和為止。然後，我放慢了腳步，感受和
品味此時此景所賦予我的種種樂趣。三點了，我從鐘樓經
過時教堂的鐘響了。此刻的美，就在於漸漸降臨的朦朧，
在於緩緩沉落、光綫漸暗的太陽。我離桑費爾德有一哩
路，在一條小徑中走着。這條小徑，夏日以野薔薇著名，
秋天以堅果和黑莓著名；即使現在，也還是有一些好像是
珊瑚珍品的薔薇果和山楂。但在冬日裏，這兒最令人賞心
悅目的，是絕對的僻靜和無葉的安寧。哪怕吹起一絲的微
風，這兒也不會發出一點聲音；因為沒有一株冬青，沒有
一株常青樹可以沙沙作響。光禿禿的山楂樹和榛樹叢，就
像鋪在小路中間的碎白石一樣地寂靜無聲。小路兩旁，極

there were only fields, where no cattle now browsed; and the little brown birds, which stirred occasionally in the hedge, looked like single russet leaves that had forgotten to drop.

Charlotte Brontë: <u>Jane Eyre</u>

目望去，只有田野，現在沒有牛在吃草，幾隻褐色的小鳥偶爾在樹籬中撲動，望去彷彿是幾片忘了落下的單片枯葉。

（英）夏洛蒂·勃朗特：《簡·愛》

22　A Bitter Black Frost

It was towards the end of February, in that year, and a bitter black[1] frost had lasted for many weeks. The keen east wind had long since swept the streets clean, though on a gusty day the dust would rise like pounded ice, and make people's faces quite smart with the cold force with which it blew against them. Houses, sky, people, and every thing looked as if a gigantic brush had washed them all over with a dark shade of Indian ink[2]. There was some reason for this grimy appearance on human beings, whatever there might be for the dun looks of the landscape; for soft water had become an article not even to be purchased; and the poor washerwomen might be seen vainly trying to procure a little by breaking the thick grey ice that coated the ditches and ponds in the neighbourhood. People prophesied a long continuance to this already lengthened frost; said the spring would be very late; no spring fashions required; no summer clothing purchased for a short uncertain summer. Indeed there was no end to the evil[3] prophesied during the continuance of that bleak east wind.

Elizabeth Gaskell: Mary Barton

1.　black：極度的。

二十二　嚴寒

　　那年二月底，一場酷寒持續了好幾個星期。強烈的東風一直吹颳着，早就把街道蕩滌得乾乾淨淨；可是遇上有陣風的天氣，灰塵被颳上天空，夾雜着一股寒氣，像冰屑般向人襲來，使臉上感到刺痛。房子、天空、人們、每樣東西看上去都像是被一把大刷子塗上了一層黑墨水。大地一片暗褐的色調自不待言，人們的嘴臉污穢不堪也都事出有因的：因為清水出錢也買不到。可憐的洗衣婦們，用盡辦法想敲碎附近溝渠和池塘上結得厚厚實實的灰色冰塊，從中取點水用，也都徒勞。大家都預測，這場已經持續了許久的嚴寒還將繼續，春天將姍姍來遲。春衣不必縫置了；夏季短暫而變幻莫測，也無需購置夏裝。真的，只要寒冷的東風滯留不去，這場人們預料中的惡劣天氣就不會有完的時日。

　　　　　　　　　　　　　（英）蓋斯凱爾夫人：《瑪麗·巴頓》

2.　Indian ink：墨汁、墨。
3.　the evil：指寒流。

Day and Night
晝夜

23 The Fresh Aurora

And now a thousand kinds of little painted birds began to warble in the trees, and with their blithe and jocund notes they seemed to welcome and salute the fresh Aurora[1], who already was showing her beautiful countenance through the gates and balconies of the East, shaking from her tresses countless liquid pearls. The plants, bathing in that fragrant moisture, seemed likewise to shed a spray of tiny white gems, the willow trees distilled sweet manna, the fountains laughed, the brooks murmured, and the meadows clad themselves in all their glory[2] at her coming.

Cervantes: Don Quixote

---

1. Aurora：羅馬神話中的曙光女神。
2. in all their glory：它們最開心得意、最漂亮壯麗的樣子。

二十三　曙光女神

　　這時，成百上千種色彩斑爛的鳥兒，在樹上婉轉啁啾，用牠們無憂無慮的歡快歌聲，招呼迎接鮮艷明麗的阿羅拉。此刻，她已經在東方的大門和陽台上露出嬌艷的臉龐，又從秀髮裏搖落無數的晶瑩水珠兒。百草沐浴着芬芳的晨露，彷彿也冒出一層白蒙蒙的細珠子。這時，楊柳滴着甘露，泉水在歡唱，小溪在低吟，草地盛裝打扮起來，歡迎她的來臨。

（西）塞萬提斯：《唐吉訶德》

24　The Invisible Sun

Next morning the not-yet-subsided sea rolled in long slow billows of mighty bulk, and striving in the Pequod's gurgling track[1], pushed her on like giants' palms outspread. The strong, unstaggering breeze abounded so, that sky and air seemed vast outbellying[2] sails; the whole world boomed before the wind. Muffled in the full morning light, the invisible sun was only known by the spread intensity of his place; where his bayonet rays moved on in stacks. Emblazonings[3], as of crowned Babylonian kings and queens, reigned over everything. The sea was as a crucible of molten gold, that bubblingly leaps with light and heat.

Long maintaining an enchanted silence, Ahab[4] stood apart; and every time the teetering ship loweringly pitched down her bowsprit, he turned to eye the bright sun's rays produced ahead; and when she profoundly settled by the stern,

---

1. gurgling track：指船在航行中在水面劃出痕迹，發出汨汨水聲。
2. outbellying：挺胸凸肚的，鼓脹着肚子的，比喻鼓得很大的風帆，形象生動有趣。

二十四　晨曦中的太陽

　　第二天早晨，在還沒有完全平靜的大海裏，大片大片的浪濤在徐徐翻動着，汩汩地沖擊着航行中的"裴廓德號"，像是一雙張開着的巨人手掌，在推着它前進。強勁的海風不斷地吹颺着，海空彷彿一張鼓着肚子的大風帆；整個世界都在風中隆隆地航行着。那個看不見的太陽，完全掩在一片晨曦之中，只有憑它四射的光芒才能確定它的位置。它那白刃般的光芒一束束往前投射，彷彿巴比倫國王和王后的寶冠上閃爍的光輝，金光燦燦地籠罩着世上萬物。大海像是一隻熔金的坩堝，嗦嗦地沸騰着光和熱。

　　亞哈站在那裏，久久一言不發，像是着了迷。每當那條起伏不定的船隻的船首斜桁往下一沉，他便望着前方那燦爛的陽光；等到船尾深深下沉，他就轉過身去察看太陽

---

3. emblazonings：原義"飾以紋章；用鮮艷的顏色裝飾"，表示炫耀，
　　頌揚之意。這裏喻指太陽發出的光芒。

4. Ahab：故事主人公亞哈船長。

he turned behind, and saw the sun's rearward place, and how the same yellow rays were blending with his undeviating wake[5].

Herman Melville: <u>Moby Dick</u>

---

5. undeviating wake：undeviating 意為 "不偏不倚"；wake 指船或其他物體在水上留下反光的痕迹。

在後面的位置，看看那同一股黃澄澄的光輝，是如何跟他
那不偏不斜的水影混合為一體的。

（美）麥爾維爾：《白鯨》

25　The Sun Rose

As the sun rose and sent his level beams along the stream, the thin stratum of mist, or malaria, rose also and dispersed, but the light was not able to enliven the dull water nor give any hint of its apparently fathomless depth. Venerable mudturtles crawled up and roosted upon the old logs in the stream, their backs glistening in the sun, the first inhabitants of the metropolis to begin the active business of the day.

Mark Twain: The Gilded Age

二十五　初升的太陽

　　太陽出來了，它那平直的光綫沿着水面投射過來，河面上升起了一層薄霧，不然就是一層瘴氣，又慢慢散了開去。但無論如何，這點光綫既不能使沉寂暗淡的河水變得活躍起來，也不能把河水像是無底的深度給映照出來。古老可敬的烏龜從水裏爬了出來，棲息在河裏漂着的圓木上，它們的背殼在太陽底下閃閃發光。在全城的居民中，它們是最早開始一日的活動的。

　　　　　　　　　　　　(美) 馬克・吐溫：《鍍金時代》

26　Morning Light

The town was glad with morning light; places that had shown ugly and distrustful all night long, now wore a smile; and sparkling sun-beams dancing on chamber windows, and twinkling through blind and curtain before sleepers' eyes, shed light even into dreams, and chased away the shadows of the night. Birds in hot rooms[1], covered up close and dark, felt it was morning, and chafed and grew restless in their little cells; bright-eyed mice crept back to their tiny homes and nestled timidly together; the sleek house-cat, forgetful of her prey, sat winking at the rays of sun starting[2] through keyhole and cranny in the door, and longed for her stealthy run and warm sleek[3] bask outside. The nobler beasts confined in dens[4] stood motionless behind their bars, and gazed on fluttering boughs and sunshine peeping through some little window, with eyes in which old forests gleamed — then trod

---

1. hot rooms = hot house，溫室
2. starting：原義 "突來"、"伸出"，這裏喻指陽光突然從門、窗的縫隙間照射進來。
3. sleek：原義 "油亮的"，這裏轉義 "舒適的"。
4. dens：栓馬的屋子，廐。

二十六　晨曦

　　晨曦給小鎮帶來了歡樂；整夜裏醜陋不堪和讓人生疑的地方，現在都泛起了笑容。燦爛的陽光在臥室的窗子上舞動，透過百葉窗和窗簾，照到睡着的人的眼睛上，甚至照進了他們的夢裏，驅走了黑夜的陰影。暖房裏的小鳥，雖然給蓋得密密實實，一片黑暗，也感知到了早晨的來臨，在牠們的小室裏變得躁動不安；眼睛烏亮的老鼠爬回牠們的小房子，怯生生地蜷伏在一起；皮毛光滑的貓兒，忘卻了自己的獵物，蹲在地上，對着從匙眼和門縫中透進來的陽光眨眼，急着想溜出去曝日取暖。圈在馬廐裏面高等一些的動物靜靜地立在柵欄後面，眼睛凝視着搖動的樹枝和從一些小窗中透了進來的陽光。在牠們的眼中，老樹林也閃閃發光了；接着，牠們那被禁錮的蹄子，在自己踏

impatiently the track their prisoned feet had worn - and stopped and gazed again. Men in their dungeons stretched their cramped cold limbs and cursed the stone[5] that no bright sky could warm. The flowers that sleep by night, opened their gentle eyes and turned them to the day. The light, creation's mind, was everywhere, and all things owned[6] its power.

Charles Dickens: <u>The Old Curiosity Shop</u>

---

5. stone：指地牢的石牆。

6. owned：這裏不作 "擁有" 解而解作 "承認"。

出的蹄窩裏不耐煩地踩動着——於是，又停了下來，再凝望。在地牢裏的囚徒伸展着他們冰冷發麻的四肢，咒罵着那堵沒有一個晴天能夠溫暖過來的石牆。夜晚沉睡的花兒張開了它們溫柔的眼睛，望着白晝。造化的光輝無所不在，天地萬物都承認它的偉大力量。

(英) 狄更斯：《老古玩店》

27 The Bright, Balmy Morning of Summer

The sun shone from out the clear blue sky, the water sparkled beneath his rays, and the trees looked greener and the flowers more gay beneath his cheering influence. The water rippled on with a pleasant sound; the trees rustled in the light wind that murmured among their leaves; the birds sang upon the boughs; and the lark carolled on high her welcome to the morning. Yes, it was morning — the bright, balmy[1] morning of summer; the minutest leaf, the smallest blade of grass, was instinct with[2] life. The ant crept forth to her daily toil, the butterfly fluttered and basked in the warm rays of the sun; myriads of insects spread their transparent wings and revelled in their brief but happy existence. Man walked forth, elated with the scene; and all was brightness and splendour.

Charles Dickens: The Pickwick Papers

---

1. balmy：柔和的，芳香的。
2. was instinct with：充滿（＝ was imbued with 或 was excited by）

二十七　夏季早晨

　　藍天清澈，太陽發出燦爛的光芒，水在陽光下閃閃發亮。在陽光的鼓舞下，樹望去比平時更加翠綠，花兒顯得更加色彩繽紛。水發出歡快聲潺潺地流去；樹在沙沙作響，微風在樹葉叢中喁喁私語；鳥兒在枝頭啁啾；雲雀高歌歡唱，迎接早晨的來臨。是的，那是早晨——明亮，香氣四溢的早晨；最最細小的葉，最最微小的草，都充滿了生機。螞蟻爬出來做牠們每日的勞作，蝴蝶撲騰着翅膀，在沐浴着溫暖的陽光；數不清的昆蟲張開牠們透明的翼，盡情地享受牠們短暫生命的歡樂。人們為這片景象感到歡欣鼓舞，得意洋洋地朝前走；一切都是光明燦爛的。

　　　　　　　　　(英) 狄更斯：《匹克威克外傳》

28 The Dead Noonday Heat

Half an hour later he was disappearing behind the Douglas mansion on the summit of Cardiff Hill and the schoolhouse was hardly distinguishable away off in the valley behind him. He entered a dense wood, picked his pathless way to the center of it, and sat down on a mossy spot under a spreading oak. There was not even a zephyr[1] stirring; the dead[2] noonday heat had even stilled the songs of the birds; nature lay in a trance that was broken by no sound but the occasional far-off hammering of a woodpecker, and this seemed to render the pervading silence and sense of loneliness the more profound.

Mark Twain: The Adventures of Tom Sawyer

---

1. zephyr：詩歌用語，微風，和風。
2. dead：死氣沉沉的，呆滯的，這裏用來描繪中午的炎熱既確切，又生動，給人一種悶得發暈之感，也跟下一句整個大自然處於 "昏睡狀態之中" 相呼應。

二十八　中午的悶熱

　　半小時之後，他就在加的夫山山頂的道格拉斯大房子
後面消失了。學校已經在背後遠遠的山谷裏，幾乎分辨不
清。他走進了一座茂密的樹林，小心翼翼地在沒有小路的
叢林中穿行，向樹林的中心走去。在一棵枝繁葉茂的橡樹
底下一塊長滿了青苔的地方坐了下來。這時候，沒有一絲
微風在攪動樹葉；中午昏沉的悶熱甚至使鳥兒都不叫了。
大自然處在昏睡狀態之中，除了偶爾從遠處傳來幾聲啄木
鳥的得得聲之外，再也沒有甚麼動靜打破這種昏睡，這就
似乎更加深了到處彌漫的沉寂和孤單。

　　　　　　　　（美）馬克・吐溫：《湯姆・索耶歷險記》

29   The Fiery Windows

Through some of the fiery windows, beautiful from without, and set, at this sunset hour, not in dull-grey stone but in a glorious house of gold, the light excluded at other windows pours in, rich, lavish[1], overflowing like the summer plenty[2] in the land[3].

Charles Dickens: <u>Bleak House</u>

---

1. lavish：奢華的，喻指陽光顯出繽紛的色彩。
2. summer plenty：喻指夏季田野中五顏六色一片豐收的景象。
3. 語法上，整段是一個部分倒裝句，句子的主要骨幹為："Through windows the light pours in"，其他皆為附加的各種修飾成分。

二十九　窗上的陽光

　　在夕陽西下時刻，陽光照在窗戶上，映出了一片霞紅，從外面看去非常美麗。這些窗戶彷彿不是裝在灰沉沉的石頭牆上，而是裝在金壁輝煌的宮殿裏。陽光就是透過這些沒有遮擋的窗戶瀉進屋裏來的，顯得色彩繽紛、絢麗多姿，滿溢得像是夏季遍地豐收的樣子。

　　　　　　　　　　（英）狄更斯：《荒涼山莊》

30 A Picture Writing on the Sun

We sat looking off across the country, watching the sun go down. The curly grass about us was on fire now. The bark of the oaks turned red as copper. There was a shimmer of gold on the brown river. Out in the stream the sandbars glittered like glass, and the light trembled in the willow thickets as if little flames were leaping among them. The breeze sank to stillness. In the ravine a ringdove mourned plaintively, and somewhere off in the bushes an owl hooted. The girls sat listless, leaning against each other. The long fingers of the sun[1] touched their foreheads.

Presently we saw a curious thing: There were no clouds, the sun was going down in a limpid, gold-washed sky. Just as the lower edge of the red disk rested on the high fields against the horizon, a great black figure suddenly appeared on the face of the sun. We sprang to our feet, straining our eyes toward it. In a moment we realized what it was. On some upland farm, a plough had been left standing in the

---

1.　The long fingers of the sun：比喻夕陽斜照時長長的光綫。

三十　太陽上的畫

　　我們坐在那裏，越過原野注視着太陽西沉。這會兒，我們周圍捲曲的牧草像着了火似的，橡樹皮紅得如紫銅，褐色的河面上泛着一層金光。遠處溪流裏，沙洲像玻璃似地閃爍着，而柳樹叢裏顫動着的光，彷彿跳躍其間的火燄。微風靜止下來了，山谷裏一隻花尾巴林鴿在哀婉地啼鳴，遠處甚麼地方的灌木叢中，一隻貓頭鷹在嚎叫。姑娘們沒精打采地相互依偎着坐在那裏，太陽的長手指撫摸着她們的額頭。

　　不一會兒，我們目睹了一件稀奇古怪的事情：天上沒有一絲雲彩，太陽在一片鍍了金似的清澄天空中下降。正當這個通紅圓盤的底邊緊貼着地平綫，停息在高處的田野上時，太陽的表面突然閃現出一個巨大的黑影。我們都忽地站了起來，張大着眼睛注視着它，很快就弄明白了那是甚麼。在某個高處農場上，有人把一部犁杖插在地上，太

field. The sun was sinking just behind it. Magnified across the distance by the horizontal light, it stood out against the sun, was exactly contained within the circle of the disk; the handles, the tongue, the share — black against the molten red. There it was, heroic in size, a picture writing on the sun.

Even while we whispered about it, our vision disappeared; the ball[2] dropped and dropped until the red tip went beneath the earth. The fields below us were dark, the sky was growing pale, and that forgotten plough had sunk back to its own littleness somewhere on the prairie.

Willa Cather: My Ántonia

---

2. ball：通常特指地球，這裏喻指太陽。

陽恰好在它的背後沉落，來自遠處水平的落日餘暉，把它放大了，突現在太陽上，而且恰好鑲在圓盤之內；犁把、犁尖和犁頭烏烏黑黑的，印在那熔鐵似的紅色背景上，就這樣變得宏大無比，成了一幅畫在太陽上的畫。

就在我們低聲談論的時候，眼前的景色消失了；圓球往下沉，往下沉，直到通紅的圓頂落到了地底下，我們下邊的原野一片昏暗。天空變得灰白起來，那把被遺忘插在地上的犁杖，又在大草原的某個地方，漸漸地回復到它原來渺小的形態。

（美）薇拉‧凱瑟：《我的安東尼亞》

31　The Scene Had an Extraordinary Charm

The sun had got low, the golden light took a deeper tone[1], and on the mountains and the plain that stretched beneath them, the masses of purple shadow seemed to glow as richly as the places that were still exposed. The scene had an extraordinary charm. The air was almost solemnly still, and the large expanse of the landscape, with its garden-like culture and nobleness of outline, its teeming valley and delicately fretted[2] hills, its peculiarly human-looking[3] touches[4] of habitation, lay there in splendid harmony and classic grace.

Henry James: The Portrait of a Lady

---

1. tone：色調，光度。
2. fretted：精工裝飾的。
3. human-looking：人性化的。
4. touches：特質，風格。

三十一　和諧典雅的畫面

　　太陽快下山了，金色的光綫越來越濃，籠罩在綿延的羣山和山腳下的平原上大塊大塊的紫色陰影，彷彿和沒有陰影的空曠地一樣，閃出絢麗的光芒。景色異常優美，空氣寧靜而蕭穆。寬闊的大地，既有園林之美，又有雄偉之勢。富饒的谷地，精美的山巒，那富有特殊生活氣息的居所，都交織出一幅和諧典雅的畫面。

　　　　　（美）亨利·詹姆斯：《一位女士的畫像》

32　The Sunset

The sunset was merely a flush of rose on a dome of silver with oak twigs and thin poplar branches against it, but a silo on the horizon changed from a red tank to a tower of violet misted over with gray. The purple road vanished, and without lights, in the darkness of a world destroyed, they swayed on — toward nothing.

Sinclair Lewis: Main Street

When the sun went down it turned all the broad river to a national banner[1] laid in gleaming bars of gold and purple and crimson; and in time these glories faded out in the twilight and left the fairy archipelagoes reflecting their fringing foliage in the steely mirror of the stream.

Mark Twain: The Gilded Age

---

1. national banner：國旗；這裏指美國星條國旗（Star-Spangled Banner）。

三十二　落日餘暉

　　在銀灰色的蒼穹上，落日只剩下一抹玫瑰色的餘暉，掩映着橡樹細嫩的樹枝，和白楊纖細的枝條。遠處地平綫上，一座穀倉由像是紅色的大水箱變成一座高高的紫色塔峯，隱沒在灰蒙蒙的霧靄裏。紫色的大路在眼前消失了，黑燈瞎火，他們的馬車在一個破滅的黑暗世界裏，搖搖晃晃地朝着一個茫然的世界往前走。

　　　　　　　　　　（美）辛克萊·路易斯：《大街》

　　落日的餘暉把這片寬廣的河水變成了一面色彩艷麗的國旗。旗面有一道道金色、紫色、紅色的條紋閃閃發光；不一會兒，這片壯麗的景象就在蒼蒼的暮色中慢慢消失，在鋼灰色的平靜水面上，只剩下羣島沿岸的樹木的倒影。

　　　　　　　　　　（美）馬克·吐溫：《鍍金時代》

33   The Two Luminaries Confronted Each Other

As we walked homeward across the fields, the sun dropped and lay like a great golden globe in the low west. While it hung there, the moon rose in the east, as big as a cart-wheel, pale silver and streaked with rose colour, thin as a bubble or a ghost-moon. For five, perhaps ten minutes, the two luminaries confronted each other across the level land, resting on opposite edges of the world.

In that singular light every little tree and shock of wheat, every sunflower stalk and clump of snow-on-the-mountain[1], drew itself up high and pointed; the very clods and furrows in the fields seemed to stand up sharply. I felt the old pull of the earth, the solemn magic that comes out of those fields at nightfall. I wished I could be a little boy again, and that my way could end there.

Willa Cather: My Ántonia

---

1.   snow-on-the-mountain：美國西部出產的銀邊草。

三十三 日月交輝

　　我們穿過田野，向回家方向走去。太陽沉落下去，像一個碩大的金球，低低地垂在西邊的天空。當它還逗留在那裏的時刻，月亮從東邊升起，大得如車輪一般，銀白色的圓面上有玫瑰色的斑紋；薄得像水泡或幻影。有五分鐘，也許十分鐘之久，這兩個燦爛的發光體在地平綫上遙遙相對，停歇在世界相反的兩端。

　　在這奇特的光照下，每一棵小樹，每一堆麥綑，每一株向日葵，和每一叢千日草，都高高地挺立着，把自己突現了出來；田野的泥塊和犂溝也都輪廓分明，我感覺到了舊日土地的吸引力，那種黃昏時分來自田野的莊嚴的魔力。我真希望我能重新做一個小男孩，希望我的道路就在此結束。

　　　　　　　　（美）薇拉・凱瑟：《我的安東尼亞》

34 One of Those Still Moments

The sun was going down. Every open evening, the hills of Derbyshire were blazed over with red sunset. Mrs. Morel watched the sun sink from the glistening sky, leaving a soft flower-blue overhead, while the western space went red, as if all the fire had swum down there, leaving the bell cast flawless blue[1]. The mountain-ash berries across the field stood fierily out from the dark leaves, for a moment. A few shocks of corn in a corner of the fallow[2] stood up as if alive; she imagined them bowing; perhaps her son would be a Joseph. In the east, a mirrored sunset floated pink opposite the west's scarlet. The big haystacks on the hillside, that butted[3] into the glare, went cold.

With Mrs. Morel it was one of those still moments when the small frets vanish, and the beauty of things stands out,

---

1. leaving... flawless blue：這個分詞短語跟前面的 "leaving a soft..." 有二種修辭效果：一是由兩個 leaving 構成的平行修辭法；二是兩個末尾詞 blue 的重複修辭法，這一用法使得句子有首尾呼應之感。

2. fallow：（農業用語）＝ fallow field，休耕地。

3. butted：原義"頂撞"。"that butted into the glare" 指乾禾堆好像插進了強光裏，意思是被太陽強光曝曬的。

三十四　最靜謐的時刻

夕陽在西沉，一到晴朗的傍晚，鮮紅的太陽就把德比郡的山巒映得紅彤彤的。穆爾太太凝望着太陽從閃亮的天空中沉落，在上空留下一片淡淡的藍色。而西邊的蒼穹一片鮮紅，好像所有的火都跑到了那邊去燃燒，使得鐘樓的外觀呈現出純淨無瑕的藍色。片刻間，田野那邊山梨樹火紅的漿果，在幽暗的樹葉中清晰可辨。休耕地一角立着的幾堆玉米幹，像是甚麼活着的東西；她想像它們正在向她鞠躬致意。説不定她的兒子會成為約瑟夫那樣的人呢！東邊的天際，在夕陽的映照下泛着玫瑰色，和西邊的緋紅遙相輝映。山坡上，給太陽曬熱的乾禾堆已經涼了下來。

對穆爾太太來説，這是最靜謐的時刻。在這種時刻，那些煩人的瑣事煙消雲散，而美好的事物躍現眼前，她心

and she had the peace and the strength to see herself. Now and again, a swallow cut close to her. Now and again[4], Annie came up with a handful of alder-currants[5]. The baby was restless on his mother's knee, clambering with his hands at the light.

D.H. Lawrence: Sons and Lovers

4. Now and again... ：這句和前面一句中，兩個 Now and again 是一種句首重複修辭法的例子。
5. alder-currants ：一種小而無核的葡萄乾。

中恢復了平靜和力量，使她能夠重新看到自己。燕子時而在她身旁飛擦而過；安妮時而手捧一把紅醋栗走過來。嬰兒在她母親的膝上躁動不安，兩隻小手在暮色中使勁揮動。

(英) 勞倫斯：《兒子和情人》

35 The Prospect

As I moved away from them along the terrace, I could not help observing how steadily they both sat gazing on the prospect, and how it thickened and closed around them. Here and there, some early lamps were seen to twinkle in the distant city; and in the eastern quarter of the sky the lurid light still hovered. But, from the greater part of the broad valley interposed, a mist was rising like a sea, which, mingling with the darkness, made it seem as if the gathering waters would encompass them. I have reason to remember this, and think of it with awe; for before I looked upon those two again, a stormy sea had risen to their feet.

Charles Dickens: David Copperfield

三十五　山谷暮色

　　當我順着平台離開她們的時候，我不禁注意到：她們兩人都是一動不動地坐在那裏，眼睛直愣愣地盯着遠處的景物。在那片景物上，暮色越來越濃，漸漸地把她們四面籠罩住了。這兒那兒，幾處亮得早些的燈火星星點點地在城市遠處閃爍；東邊這方夜空，濃烈的霞光依舊流連。但是，在介乎這兒和城市之間這一大片空曠的低谷裏，霧像海洋似地攏了過來。這片霧靄與暮色混合，看着彷彿洪水匯聚，會把她們吞沒。那景象，我是永遠不會忘卻的，每逢想起，就有一種敬畏之情。因為，當我又回眸去看她們兩個的時候，只見波濤洶湧的霧海，已經翻滾到她們的腳下了。

　　　　　　　　　　　　（英）狄更斯：《大衛·科波菲爾》

36   The Evening Star

There had been a warm thaw all day, with mushy yards
and little streams of dark water gurgling cheerfully into the
streets out of old snow-banks. My window was open, and
the earthy wind blowing through made me indolent. On the
edge of the prairie, where the sun had gone down, the sky
was turquoise blue, like a lake, with gold light throbbing in
it. Higher up, in the utter clarity of the western slope, the
evening star hung like a lamp suspended by silver chains —
like the lamp engraved upon the title-page of old Latin texts,
which is always appearing in new heavens, and waking new
desires in men.

Willa Cather: My Ántonia

三十六　晚星

　　整天都是一種和暖的冰雪融化的天氣，院子裏泥濘糊糊，從舊日的雪堆上淌出的黑水匯成歡快的溪流，淙淙地向大街上流去。我的窗子敞着，帶着泥土氣息的風從窗口吹進來，讓我感到懶洋洋的。在太陽沉落的草原邊緣，天空清澄碧藍，像一汪湖水，博動着粼粼金光。再往上，西邊明淨的蒼穹裏，晚星像一盞用銀鏈子懸掛在天空的明燈——像是印在舊時拉丁文課本扉頁上的那盞明燈。那盞燈總是出現在新的天空，喚起人們心中新的慾望。

　　　　　　　　　　　(美)　薇拉‧凱瑟：《我的安東尼亞》

37 Midnight Dark

I lingered at the gates; I lingered on the lawn; I paced backwards and forwards on the pavement: the shutters of the glass door were closed; I could not see into the interior; and both my eyes and spirit seemed drawn from the gloomy house — from the gray hollow filled with rayless cells, as it appeared to me — to that sky expanded before me — a blue sea absolved from taint of cloud; the moon ascending it in solemn march, her orb[1] seeming to look up as she left the hilltops, from behind which she had come, far and farther below her, and aspired to the zenith, midnight dark in its fathomless depth and measureless distance; and for those trembling stars that followed her course, they made my heart tremble, my veins glow when I viewed them. Little things recall us to earth[2]: the clock struck in the hall; that sufficed. I turned from moon and stars, opened a side-door, and went in.

Charlotte Brontë: Jane Eyre

---

1. orb：一般指球體，特別是天上的圓球體；可解作"眼睛"、"眼球"；也可指西方帝王手執代表權力的金球。

三十七　午夜的蒼穹

　　我在大門口徜徉，我在草坪上徜徉，我在門前小石徑上來回踱步。玻璃門的門扇已經關上，我無法看到裏面；何況，此刻我的眼睛和心彷彿都已經被吸引開了那所陰暗的住屋——離開了那個在我看來滿是昏暗小密室的灰色洞穴——轉向那個展現在我面前的蒼穹——一片沒有一絲雲彩的藍色海洋。月亮從山頂背後，很低很低的地方，邁着莊嚴的步伐開始登場，她彷彿眼望着上方，渴望着一直達到天之巔，達到那個深不可測、遠不可量的午夜漆黑一片的地方。而那些追隨着她的熠熠繁星，仰望着它們就使我的心兒發顫，血管裏熱血奔騰。些微小事就足以把我們召回大地；大廳裏的鐘敲響了，那就足夠。我從月亮和星星那兒轉過頭來，打開一扇邊門，走了進去。

　　　　　　　　　　(英) 夏洛蒂·勃朗特：《簡·愛》

---

2. recall us to earth：earth 這裏語帶相關，指"地上"或"現實"
　　表示從觀看天上回轉到地上，從暇思返回現實環境。

38   The Beauty of the Night

The beauty of the night made him want to shout. A half-moon, dusky gold, was sinking behind the black sycamore at the end of the garden, making the sky dull purple with its glow. Nearer, a dim white fence of lilies went across the garden, and the air all round seemed to stir with scent, as if it were alive. He went across the bed of pinks, whose keen perfume came sharply across the rocking[1], heavy scent of the lilies, and stood alongside the white barrier of flowers. They flagged all loose, as if they were panting. The scent made him drunk. He went down to the field to watch the moon sink under.

A corncrake in the hay-close called insistently. The moon slid quite quickly downwards, growing more flushed[2]. Behind him the great flowers leaned as if they were calling. And then, like a shock, he caught another perfume, something raw and coarse. Hunting round, he found the purple iris, touched their fleshy throats and their dark, grasping hands[3].

---

1. rocking：蕩漾；這裏指發出陣陣香氣。
2. flushed：發紅；這裏指月色變深。

三十八　月色花香

　　夜色之美使他真想大聲呼喊。一輪暗黃的半月正從園
子盡頭的一棵黑黑的無花果樹的背後沉落下去，在天際留
下一片暗淡的紫輝。近處，一排白百合像一道朦朧的柵欄
橫過花園。周圍空氣中香氣四溢，彷彿充滿着生命。他穿
過一片粉紅色的花叢，站在那道白色花牆旁邊。粉紅色花
朵的香味頓時撲鼻而來，一時蓋過了白色百合花的陣陣濃
郁的香氣。花兒都柔軟無力地垂了下來，好像在喘大氣一
般。花香使他沉醉，他向田野走去，看着月亮慢慢下沉。

　　附近乾草堆裏，一隻秧雞不停地叫着。月亮在很快沉
落下去，月色變得越來越濃。他身後，那些美好的花兒傾
斜着，像是在呼喚他。忽然間，像是一陣震盪，他又聞到
另一股香味，這是種又生又粗的東西的氣味。他在四處尋
找，發現了一些紫鳶尾花。於是，他伸手去觸摸它們那些
多肉的 "喉部" ，和那些深色的，像貪婪攫取的手。無論

3.　fleshy throats and... grasping hands：都是比喻鳶尾花 "花枝招
　　展" ，發出誘人的形態。

At any rate, he had found something. They stood stiff in the darkness. Their scent was brutal. The moon was melting down upon the crest of the hill. It was gone; all was dark. The corncrake called still.

D.H. Lawrence: <u>Sons and Lovers</u>

如何，他還是找到了一些東西。它們在黑暗中直挺挺地站立着，其氣味帶着野性。月亮已沉入山頭背後，逐漸消失了；到處是一片黑暗。那隻秧雞還在叫。

(英) 勞倫斯：《兒子和情人》

39 Moonlight Beauty

In passing Fieldhead, on her return, its moonlight beauty attracted her glance, and stayed her step an instant. Tree and hall rose peaceful under the night sky and clear full orb; pearly paleness gilded the building; mellow brown gloom bosomed it round; shadows of deep green brooded above its oak-wreathed roof. The broad pavement in front shone pale also; it gleamed as if some spell had transformed the dark granite to glistering Parian[1].

Charlotte Brontë: Shirley

---

1. Parian：希臘 Paros 島出產的著名的白色大理石。

三十九　美好的月色

　　在回家途中，路過菲爾哈德的時候，她的目光被美好的月色吸引住了，一時她收住了腳步。大樹和宅第靜穆地佇立在夜空和明澈的圓月下面；月光給那幢建築鍍上了一層珍珠似的蒼白色；四周幽暗而柔和的褐色把它環抱着；深綠色的陰影籠罩着它那被橡樹花冠覆蓋的屋頂。門前寬闊的地面也是白晃晃的，閃出熠熠的光輝，彷彿有人使了魔法，把那黝黑的花崗石變成了光彩奪目的大理石。

（英）夏洛蒂·勃朗特：《謝利》

40 The Moonlight

Along the road the shadows from oak-branches were inked on the snow like bars of music. Then the sled came out on the surface of Lake Minniemashie. Across the thick ice was a veritable road, a short-cut for farmers. On the glaring expanse of the lake — levels of hard crust, flashes of green ice blown clear, chains of drifts ribbed like the sea-beach — the moonlight was overwhelming. It stormed on the snow, it turned the woods ashore into crystals of fire. The night was tropical and voluptuous. In that drugged magic[1] there was no difference between heavy heat and insinuating cold.

Sinclair Lewis: Main Street

---

1. drugged magic：drugged 原義 ˮ麻醉ˮ ；magic 這裏指一種神秘迷幻的美。

四十 月光

　　沿着大路兩旁，橡樹枝條投在雪地上的影子如同樂譜
上一節節的音符一般。不一會兒，雪橇駛出了大路，來到
了明尼瑪西湖面上。農夫喜歡抄近路，從結得厚實的冰層
上駛過去，倒是一條實實在在的捷徑。月光宛如高山瀑
布，傾瀉在這一望無際的眩目的湖面上——傾瀉在一堆堆
堅硬的冰層上，傾瀉在塊塊清澈光潔，泛着綠光的冰丘
上；傾瀉在像波濤連湧的海灘般的條條隆起的雪堆上。月
光熾烈，照射在雪地上，把湖畔的小樹林變成了像火般耀
眼的水晶。這像是個富於熱帶情調令人心往神馳的夜晚。
在這令人沉醉的美景裏，酷暑與嚴寒幾無多大區別了。

　　　　　　　　　　　(美) 辛克萊·路易斯：《大街》

41　The Perfectly Round Moon

The moon, dark red and perfectly round, was just climbing above the horizon, beyond the meadows. It rose swiftly behind the poplars, whose branches partially hid it like a torn black curtain, then it appeared in all its elegant whiteness, lighting up the cloudless sky; finally, moving more slowly, it cast on the surface of the river a large patch of light which glittered like an infinity of stars; the silvery gleam seemed to writhe all the way to the bottom of the water like a headless serpent covered with luminous scales. It also resembled a monstrous candlestick with molten diamonds streaming down its sides. The soft night enveloped them; the spaces between the leaves of the trees were filled in with dark shadows. Emma, her eyes half closed, breathed in the cool breeze with deep sighs. Lost in reverie, they did not speak. The sweetness of earlier days returned to their hearts, as abundant and silent as the flowing river, soft as the fragrance of the lilacs, and it projected into their memories longer and more melancholy shadows than those cast on the grass by the motionless willows. Often some prowling nocturnal animal, a hedgehog or a weasel, would rustle through the foliage, and occasionally they heard the sound of a ripe peach dropping from one of the trees along the wall.

四十一　仲秋圓月

　　草原盡頭，一輪暗紅滾圓的月亮剛剛從天際露出臉兒，很快從白楊樹的枝葉後面升起。這些枝葉，猶如一塊撕破了的黑幕，半藏半露地將它遮了起來。接着閃出一輪圓月，素靜的白光照亮了無雲的夜空。後來它又放慢了腳步，朝河面投下一片亮光，宛如無數閃閃發光的星星。這道銀光彷彿一條遍體有閃亮的鱗片的無頭巨蛇，曲曲彎彎，一直盤到河底；又好似一隻碩大無比的蠟燭台，四周不斷往下淌着熔化了的鑽石。溫柔的夜色籠罩着他們，樹葉間佈滿了陰影。愛瑪半閉着眼睛，隨着深深的嘆息，吸進吹來的清風。他們沉浸在夢幻之中，兩人一時無語。往日的柔情，滿滿的，靜靜的，像一條小河，又流回到他們的心田；又像丁香花一樣，散發着醉人的芬芳。這股柔情在他們的記憶中投下的影子，比靜止的柳樹投在草地上的影子更長更陰鬱。他們不時聽到有刺蝟，或者黃鼠狼這類夜行動物在枝葉間穿行，發出沙沙的聲響。有時還聽見一隻熟透了的桃子，從牆邊的樹上掉了下來。

"What a beautiful night!" said Rodolphe.

"We'll have others[1]!" replied Emma.

Gustave Flaubert: <u>Madame Bovary</u>

---

1. "We'll have others!" ： 這裏 others = other beautiful nights like this.

"啊！多麼美麗的夜晚！"魯道耳夫說。

"我們往後會有許多這樣的夜晚！"愛瑪答道。

(法) 福樓拜：《包法利夫人》

42　The Wild Moon

It was a murky confusion — here and there blotted with a color like the color of the smoke from damp fuel — of flying clouds, tossed up into most remarkable heaps, suggesting greater heights in the clouds than there were depths below them to the bottom of the deepest hollows in the earth, through which the wild moon seemed to plunge headlong, as if, in a dread disturbance of the laws of nature, she had lost her way and were frightened. There had been a wind all day; and it was rising then, with an extraordinary great sound. In another hour it had much increased, and the sky was more overcast, and it blew hard.

But, as the night advanced, the clouds closing in and densely overspreading the whole sky, then very dark, it came on to[1] blow, harder and harder. It still increased, until our horses could scarcely face the wind. Many times, in the dark part of the night (it was then late in September, when the nights were not short), the leaders turned about, or came to a dead stop; and we were often in serious apprehension that

---

1.　came on to：開始，如："It came on to snow." 開始下雪。

四十二　失常的月亮

　　天上一片烏黑混亂，這裏那裏塗滿了像濕柴冒出的那種黑煙的顏色。亂雲飛渡，高高疊起，令人想到烏雲下面，直到地上低谷最深的谷底，其深度也遠所不及。失常的月亮好像在亂雲堆中瞎竄亂撞，彷彿在自然界規律反常的可怕混亂裏，她迷了途，受了驚。那天一整天風不停的吹，這會兒風大了起來，發出異常巨大的呼嘯聲。一小時後，風勢大大升級，天空更加陰暗，風越發起勁地颳着。

　　夜色漸濃，雲堆合攏起來，密密實實地佈滿了整個天空。那時天已漆黑一片，風也越颳越猛，風勢不斷增強，我們的馬幾乎不能再頂風前進了。在昏暗的夜色中（當時正是九月末，夜晚已經不短了），有好幾次幾匹先導馬都回轉身來，或者突然站住不動；我們一路上常常提心吊膽，

the coach would be blown over. Sweeping gusts of rain came up before this storm, like showers of steel; and, at those times, when there was any shelter of trees or lee walls to be got, we were fain[2] to stop, in a sheer impossibility of continuing the struggle.

Charles Dickens: <u>David Copperfield</u>

---

2. fain：古語或詩歌用語，解作〝樂於〞、〝欣然〞。

唯恐驛車會被風颳翻了。陣陣橫飛平掠的大雨隨風而來，都像飛刀流劍一般。那時，每逢遇到有避風的樹，或者背風的牆，我們都恨不得停下來，因為我們實在是無法繼續掙扎下去了。

（英）狄更斯：《大衛·科波菲爾》

43　Piercing Cold Night

The night was bitter cold. The snow lay on the ground, frozen into a hard thick crust, so that only the heaps that had drifted into by-ways and corners were affected by the sharp wind that howled abroad: which, as if expending increased fury on such prey as it found, caught it savagely up in clouds, and, whirling it into a thousand misty eddies, scattered it in air. Bleak, dark, and piercing cold, it was a night for the well-housed and fed to draw round the bright fire and thank God they were at home; and for the homeless, starving wretch to lay him down and die. Many hunger-worn outcasts close their eyes in our bare streets, at such times, who, let their crimes have been what they may, can hardly open them in a more bitter world.

Charles Dickens: <u>Oliver Twist</u>

四十三　寒冷徹骨的夜晚

　　這天夜晚酷寒難當。地面上的雪，已經凍成厚厚的一層冰殼，這樣，便只剩下積聚在冷清小徑和偏僻角落裏的小雪堆，承受外面咆哮的風刀霜劍的襲擊。風好像在竭盡全力，變本加厲地肆虐，粗暴地抓住了它的獵物，把它們猛烈地颳上雲端，捲成千萬團霧濛濛的旋渦，在空中飄散。在這樣淒涼、黑暗、寒冷徹骨的夜晚，吃飽穿暖，身居安樂窩的人們圍在熊熊的爐火旁，他們為此刻身在家中而感謝上帝；而那些飢寒交迫、無家可歸的人們，只有倒斃路旁。每逢這種時刻，便有許多被社會遺棄的可憐人，在飢餓之中，在我們的冷街僻巷裏閉上了眼睛。不論他們先前是否罪孽深重，誰也不可能睜開眼睛，看到一個更為悽涼的世界。

　　　　　　　　　　（英）狄更斯：《苦海孤雛》

The Weather
氣象

44　The Marsh-mist

It was a rimy morning, and very damp. I had seen the damp lying on the outside of my little window, as if some goblin had been crying there all night, and using the window for a pocket-handkerchief. Now I saw the damp lying on the bare hedges and spare grass, like a coarser sort of spiders' webs, hanging itself from twig to twig and blade to blade. On every rail and gate, wet lay clammy, and the marsh-mist was so thick that the wooden finger on the post directing people to our village — a direction which they never accepted, for they never came there — was invisible to me until I was quite close under it. Then, as I looked up at it, while it dripped, it seemed to my oppressed conscience like a phantom devoting me to the Hulks[1].

The mist was heavier yet when I got out upon the marshes, so that instead of my running at everything, everything seemed to run at me. This was very disagreeable to a guilty mind. The gates and dikes and banks came bursting at me through the mist, as if they cried as plainly as could be, "A boy with somebody else's pork pie! Stop him!" The cattle

---

1.　Hulks：歷史用語，囚船，監獄船。

四十四　沼地濃霧

　　清晨有霜，十分潮濕，早起就看見我的小窗外邊蒙着一層水氣，好像是有個妖精在那裏哭了一夜，把窗玻璃當成一塊擦眼淚的手絹了。這會兒，只見外面光禿禿的籬笆上和稀疏的小草上全都附着水氣，看上去像粗眼蜘蛛網，網絲從這根樹枝掛到那根樹枝，從這片草葉掛到那片草葉。家家圍欄上，大門上，都蒙着一團黏糊糊的濕氣。沼澤地上的霧氣更濃；我一直走到路牌跟前，才看清為來我們村的人指路的那隻手指──其實過往的人從來不聽它的，因為根本就沒有人到我們那裏去。抬頭一看，路牌在淅淅瀝瀝往下淌水，我壓抑的心靈覺得它彷彿一個幽靈，逼着我非上囚船不可。

　　可是，等我走到沼地上，霧更加濃了，朦朧之中，像是一切都在向我撲了過來，而不是我朝着甚麼目標奔過去。一個捫心有愧的人看到這般光景着實不好受。閘門、堤壩、河岸，都紛紛破霧而出，來到我面前，還好像毫不客氣地向我大聲喊："一個孩子偷了人家的肉餡餅，抓住

came upon me with like suddenness[2], staring out of their eyes, and steaming out of their nostrils, "Halloa, young thief!" One black ox, with a white cravat on — who even had to my awakened conscience something of a clerical air — fixed me so obstinately with his eyes, and moved his blunt head round in such an accusatory manner as I moved round, that I blubbered out to him, "I couldn't help it, sir! It wasn't for myself I took it!" Upon which he put down his head, blew a cloud of smoke out of his nose, and vanished with a kick-up of his hindlegs and a flourish[3] of his tail.

Charles Dickens: Great Expectations

---

2. with like suddenness：同樣地突然。
3. flourish：揮動

他！"牛羣也冷不防跟我撞了個照面，圓睜怒目，鼻孔裏冒着粗氣，叫道："啊呀，小毛賊！"一頭戴着白項圈的黑公牛（我這不安的良心看來，儼然像個牧師）頑固地盯着我，我走過去了，牠還掉轉那笨拙的腦袋，用責備的神氣瞪看我。我禁不住向牠哭訴告饒："我也是不得已的呀，大爺，這肉餡餅不是拿來給我自己吃的呀！"聽了這話，它才低下頭去，鼻子裏又噴出一團氣，後腿一抬，尾巴一捧，走開去了。

（英）狄更斯：《遠大前程》

45　A Mist Hung over the River

A mist hung over the river, deepening the red glare of
the fires that burnt upon the small craft moored off the
different wharfs, and rendering darker and more indistinct
the mirky[1] buildings on the banks. The old smoke-stained
storehouses on either side, rose heavy and dull from the dense
mass of roofs and gables[2], and frowned sternly upon water
too black to reflect even their lumbering shapes. The tower
of old Saint Saviour's Church, and the spire of Saint Magnus,
so long the giant-warders of the ancient bridge, were visible
in the gloom; but the forest of shipping below bridge, and
the thickly scattered[3] spires of churches above, were nearly
all hidden from the sight.

Charles Dickens: Oliver Twist

---

1. mirky = murky：陰暗的、模糊的。
2. gables：山牆：雙斜面屋頂形成的山形牆。
3. thickly scattered：既濃密又分散的。這是個修辭上的矛盾修飾法
   (oxymoron)。

四十五　河上夜霧

　　河上籠罩着薄霧，泊在河邊各處碼頭附近的小船上燈火的紅光因而顯得更紅。岸邊陰沉沉的建築物，也顯得更暗更朦朧。兩岸給煙薰黑的舊倉房矗立在密密麻麻的屋頂和山牆叢中，顯得笨重、呆滯，慍怒地注視着河面，彷彿責備河水太黑，連它們這樣的龐然大物也映不出來。在幽暗中，古老的救世主教堂的鐘塔，和聖馬格努斯教堂尖頂的輪廓隱約可見，它們像兩個巨大的神靈，守衛着這座歷史悠久的大橋已不知有多少個年代。然而，橋下林立的船桅和橋上分立的重重的教堂尖頂，幾乎全都湮沒在霧靄之中，難以辨認。

　　　　　　　　　　（英）狄更斯：《苦海孤雛》

46 Fog

Fog everywhere. Fog up the river, where it flows among green aits[1] and meadows; fog down the river, where it rolls defiled among the tiers of shipping, and the waterside pollutions of a great (and dirty) city. Fog on the Essex[2] Marshes, fog on the Kentish[3] heights. Fog creeping into the cabooses[4] of collier-brigs[5], fog lying out on the yards, and hovering in the rigging of great ships; fog drooping on the gunwales of barges and small boats. Fog in the eyes and throats of ancient Greenwich[6] pensioners, wheezing by the firesides of their wards; fog in the stem and bowl of the afternoon pipe of the wrathful skipper[7], down in his close cabin; fog cruelly pinching the toes and fingers of his

---

1. aits：英國用語，河、湖中的小島。
2. Essex：埃塞克斯郡，在倫敦東北方。
3. Kentish：肯特郡的；肯特郡在倫敦的東南方。
4. cabooses：英國用語，船上的廚房。
5. collier-brigs：運煤的雙桅方帆船。
6. Greenwich：格林威治區，倫敦東南的一個區，設有著名的天文台。
7. skipper：（小商船、漁船或遊艇的）船長。

四十六　霧

　　滿眼是霧，霧籠罩着河的上游，在綠色小島和草地之間飄蕩；霧籠罩着河的下游，在一排排泊着的船隻之間，在這個巨大的（骯髒的）城市污染的水域邊滾動着。霧籠罩着埃塞克斯郡的沼地，霧籠罩着肯德郡的高地。霧爬進雙桅方帆運煤船的艙面廚房；霧躺在船的帆桁上，徘徊在大船的索具之間；霧低懸在大平底船和小木船的船舷邊上。霧鑽進了那些待在格林威治區的收容所裏，靠養老金生活，圍着火爐呼哧呼哧喘息的老人的眼睛和喉嚨裏；霧鑽進了午後待在小密室裏抽煙的生氣的船長的煙管和煙斗裏，霧殘酷地折磨着站在甲板上那個哆嗦着的小學徒的手

shivering little 'prentice boy on deck. Chance people on the bridges peeping over the parapets[8] into a nether[9] sky of fog, with fog all round them, as if they were up in a balloon, and hanging in the misty clouds.

Charles Dickens: <u>Bleak House</u>

---

8. parapets：矮護牆。
9. nether：古語，詩歌用語：下面的 = lower、under。

指和腳趾。偶爾從橋上走過的人們，憑欄窺視橋下的霧
空，四周一片迷霧，恍如乘着汽球，在霧濛濛的雲端飄
蕩。

(英) 狄更斯：《荒涼山莊》

47   Gusts in Innumerable Series

It might reasonably have been supposed that she was listening to the wind, which rose somewhat as the night advanced, and laid hold of the attention. The wind, indeed, seemed made for the scene, as the scene seemed made for the hour. Part of its tone was quite special; what was heard there could be heard nowhere else. Gusts in innumerable series followed each other from the north-west, and when each one of them raced past the sound of its progress resolved into three. Treble, tenor, and bass notes were to be found therein. The general ricochet[1] of the whole over pits and prominences[2] had the gravest pitch of the chime. Next there could be heard the baritone buzz of a holly tree. Below these in force, above them in pitch, a dwindled voice strove hard at a husky tune, which was the peculiar local sound alluded

---

1.   ricochet：原指石片、子彈等的回跳，或漂掠，這裏用來比喻掠過地面呼嘯而去的整個風勢。
2.   prominences：轉義 "山岡"、"山巒"，pits and prominences：溝壑和山岡。

四十七　荒原陣風

　　要是説那個女人在聽風聲，倒不是沒有道理的推斷。
因為那時夜色漸漸深起來，風也漸漸大起來，開始惹人注
意。實在説起來，那樣的風，彷彿是為那樣的景而設的，
就如那樣的景物是為那樣的時光而設一樣。風的音調，有
一部分是相當特殊的；只能在那裏聽到，而不可能在任何
別的地方聽到。狂風從西北方颼來，無數連串，一陣緊接
一陣。每一陣風在疾速掠過的時候，風聲分解成三種音
調：高音、中音和低音都能在裏面聽出來。整個風勢掠過
坑谷，飛過岡巒，發出如同最低沉的聲音；第二種能夠聽
得出來的音調，是冬青樹颯颯作響的男中音；還有一種，
音量上低些，調門上高些，是一種從變細的嗓門擠出的粗
啞聲；剛才説過的本地獨有的聲音就是這一種。比起另外

to. Thinner and less immediately traceable than the other two, it was far more impressive than either. In it lay what may be called the linguistic[3] peculiarity of the heath; and being audible nowhere on earth off a heath, it afforded a shadow of reason for the woman's tenseness, which continued as unbroken as ever.

Thomas Hardy: The Return of the Native

---

3. linguistic：原義 "語言學上的"，這裏，將荒原上種種各具特色的風聲，比作有具體內涵的語言，由聲表意，彷彿從風聲中也可讓人領略到某種特殊的樂趣。

兩種來，雖然更加細弱，它的源頭更加難以追尋，但是，它給人留下的印象卻遠比另外兩種強烈。我們可以說，荒原上由聲表意的那種特色，也就含在這種聲音裏；既是這種聲音，除了在荒原上，在人世間任何別的地方一概難以聽到，那麼，這個女人所以側耳細聽，也許就為的是它了；而這種聚精會神在繼續着，跟以前一樣。

(英) 哈代：《還鄉》

48 The Dust

In the roads where the teams moved, where the wheels milled the ground and the hooves of the horses beat the ground, the dirt crust broke and the dust formed. Every moving thing lifted the dust into the air; a walking man lifted a thin layer as high as his waist, and a wagon lifted the dust as high as the fence tops, and an automobile boiled a cloud behind it. The dust was long in settling back again.

When June was half gone, the big clouds moved up out of Texas and the Gulf, high heavy clouds, rain-heads. The men in the fields looked up at the clouds and sniffed at them and held wet fingers up to sense the wind. And the horses were nervous while the clouds were up. The rain-heads dropped a little spattering, and hurried on to some other country. Behind them the sky was pale again and the sun flared. In the dust there were drop craters where the rain had fallen, and there were clean splashes on the corn, and that was all.

A gentle wind followed the rain clouds, driving them on northward, a wind that softly clashed the drying corn. A day went by and the wind increased, steady, unbroken by gusts. The dust from the roads fluffed up and spread out and fell on the weeds beside the fields, and fell into the fields a little

四十八　塵沙

　　在車馬往來的大路上，路面受車輪的碾磨和馬蹄的踐踏，乾結的泥塊碎裂，化成了塵土。各種活動的東西將塵土揚到了空中：走路的人揚起齊腰高一層薄薄的塵土；篷車把塵埃揚到籬笆頂端，汽車則在後面滾起團團塵霧，這些塵霧要很久很久才落下來。

　　六月過了一半，得克薩斯和墨西哥海灣上空翻滾着大塊的雲團，厚厚的，含雨的烏雲。田野上的人抬起頭來望着這些雲，用鼻子去聞聞，並伸出潤濕的手指探探風勢。天上堆着雲塊的時候，田野上的馬都有些着慌。烏雲灑下幾點雨水，便匆匆飄往其它的鄉野去了。雲飛走後，天空又恢復了一片青灰色，太陽依舊烈焰般照射着，塵土中雨點落過的地方留下了一些凹痕，玉米上有了一些澄清的水珠，這就完事了。

　　一陣微風緊追着雨雲，把它們趕往北方，輕輕地吹動着正在乾枯的玉米。一天過去了，風勢漸漸大了起來，但還算很平穩，沒有陣風。大路上的塵埃揚了起來，飄灑開後落到了田邊的野草上，落到了附近不遠的田野裏。這會

way. Now the wind grew strong and hard and it worked at the rain crust in the cornfields. Little by little the sky was darkened by the mixing dust, and the wind felt over the earth, loosened the dust, and carried it away. The wind grew stronger. The rain crust broke and the dust lifted up out of the fields and drove grey plumes into the air like sluggish smoke. The corn threshed the wind and made a dry, rushing sound. The finest dust did not settle back to earth now, but disappeared into the darkening sky.

The wind grew stronger, whisked under stones, carried up straws and old leaves, and even little clods, marking its course as it sailed across the fields. The air and the sky darkened and through them the sun shone redly, and there was a raw sting in the air. During the night the wind raced faster over the land, dug cunningly among the rootlets of the corn, and the corn fought the wind with its weakened leaves until the roots were freed by the prying wind and then each stalk settled wearily sideways toward the earth and pointed the direction of the wind[1].

John Steinbeck: The Grapes of Wrath

---

1. pointed the direction of the wind：這裏意為順着風勢的方向。

兒風勢更強更猛了，颳着玉米地裏雨後乾結的泥土，漸漸天空中彌漫着混合的塵土，天色變得陰暗。風掠過大地，弄鬆了塵土又把它颳到其它地方。風越颳越猛，雨後乾結的地面裂了開來，田野裏的塵土捲入空中，像是一道道緩緩飄動的灰色煙霧。玉米迎風撲打着，發出豁啦啦的乾燥聲。最細的塵埃現在不再落回大地，卻消失在越來越暗的空中。

風勢變得更猛烈，在石頭底下疾速掠過，捲走了稻草和枯葉，甚至小土塊，颳過田野時留下了道道蹤迹。天色昏暗，太陽已成了一團紅光，空氣裏有一種粗糙的刺痛感。夜裏，風以更快的速度掠過地面，它在玉米的根部狡猾地掘着，玉米用它柔弱的葉子跟大風搏鬥，直到根部被猛撬的風颳鬆了，結果一株株被折磨得精疲力竭的玉米，都順着風勢倒伏了下來。

（美）斯坦倍克：《憤怒的葡萄》

49 The Wind

The wind blew, not up the road or down it, though that's bad enough, but sheer across it, sending the rain slanting down like the lines they used to rule in the copy-books at school to make the boys slope[1] well. For a moment it would die away, and the traveller would begin to delude himself into the belief that, exhausted with its previous fury, it had quietly lain itself down to rest, when, whoo! he would hear it growling and whistling in the distance, and on it would come, rushing over the hill-tops and sweeping along the plain, gathering sound and strength as it drew nearer until it dashed with a heavy gust against horse and man, driving the sharp rain into their ears and its cold damp breath into their very bones; and past them it would scour, far, far away, with a stunning roar, as if in ridicule of their weakness and triumphant in the consciousness of its own strength and power.

Charles Dickens: The Pickwick Papers

---

1. slope：原義"傾斜"，這裏意為畫斜綫。

四十九　風

　　風，不是從路上迎面吹來，或者從背後吹來——固然，那已經是夠糟的了——卻是一個勁兒地橫着吹過馬路，把雨吹成斜的，就像人們在學校裏用尺畫在習字簿上讓孩子們照着寫字的斜綫似的。有一陣子，風停了下來，旅行者信以為是前面那陣疾風吹得過猛，已經精疲力竭，這會兒悄沒聲兒躺倒休息了。誰曉得，"呼"的一聲，又聽到它在遠處咆哮起來，呼嘯着捲土重來了。它疾速吹過山崗，掠過平原，風勢越吹越猛，聲音越來越大，到後來，一陣狂風向馬和人直撲了過來。刺人的雨點直往耳朵裏灌，冷冰冰的寒氣直往骨子裏鑽；風從他們身邊颳過去老遠老遠了，但還在發着震耳欲聾的吼叫，像是在嘲弄他們的怯弱，洋洋得意於自己無比的威力。

　　　　　　　　　（英）狄更斯：《匹克威克外傳》

50 The Roaring Wind and the Booming Thunderblasts

About midnight Joe awoke, and called the boys. There was a brooding oppressiveness in the air that seemed to bode something. The boys huddled themselves together and sought the friendly companionship of the fire, though the dull dead heat of the breathless atmosphere was stifling. They sat still, intent and waiting. The solemn hush continued. Beyond the light of the fire everything was swallowed up in the blackness of darkness. Presently there came a quivering glow that vaguely revealed the foliage for a moment and then vanished. By and by another came, a little stronger. Then another. Then a faint moan came sighing through the branches of the forest and the boys felt a fleeting breath upon their cheeks, and shuddered with the fancy that the Spirit of the Night had gone by. There was a pause. Now a weird flash turned night into day and showed every little grass blade, separate and distinct, that grew about their feet. And it showed three white, startled faces, too. A deep peal of thunder went rolling and tumbling down the heavens and lost itself in sullen rumblings in the distance. A sweep of chilly air passed by, rustling all the leaves and snowing the flaky ashes broadcast about the fire. Another fierce glare lit up the forest, and an instant crash

五十　風嘯雷鳴

　　約莫半夜時分，喬醒過來，叫那兩個孩子。空氣裏有一股低沉的悶熱，好像預示着天氣會有變化。雖然一絲絲風都沒有，空氣裏散發着悶人的，死氣沉沉的熱氣，令人窒息，孩子們還是偎依在一起，竭力往火堆旁靠。他們一聲不響地坐着，聚精會神地等待着甚麼。四周依然靜穆無聲，在火光照到的範圍之外，一切都被無邊的黑暗所吞沒。不久便來了一道游移的閃光，隱隱約約地照亮了樹上的枝葉，片刻之間消失了。接着又是一道閃光，比剛才的更強一點。然後又是一道，跟着聽到一陣低沉的哼哼聲，像嘆息似地從林中枝葉裏傳來。孩子們覺得有一股飛快的氣息吹到他們的臉上，便幻想着是黑夜的精靈從他們的身邊走了過去，嚇得身子瑟瑟地抖了起來。接着沉寂了一會兒，隨後又是一道鬼怪似的閃光，把黑夜照成了白晝，他們腳下的每一棵草都照得清清楚楚；同時還照亮了三張驚恐、蒼白的小臉。轟隆隆，一陣深沉的雷聲從天上一路滾下來，漸漸變成鬱悶的響聲，在遠處消失了。一陣冷颼颼的風颳了過來，吹得樹葉沙沙作響，吹得火堆裏的灰燼像雪片似地四處飛揚。又是一道強烈的閃電，把樹林照得通

followed that seemed to rend the treetops right over the boys' heads. They clung together in terror, in the thick gloom that followed. A few big raindrops fell pattering upon the leaves.

"Quick, boys! go for the tent!" exclaimed Tom.

They sprang away, stumbling over roots and among vines in the dark, no two plunging in the same direction. A furious blast roared through the trees, making everything sing as it went. One blinding flash after another came, and peal on peal of deafening thunder. And now a drenching rain poured down and the rising hurricane drove it in sheets along the ground. The boys cried out to each other, but the roaring wind and the booming thunderblasts drowned their voices utterly. However, one by one they straggled in at last and took shelter under the tent, cold, scared, and streaming with water.

Mark Twain: The Adventures of Tom Sawyer

亮，隨即就是一聲霹靂，好像就在孩子們的頭頂上把樹尖都劈成了兩半。在那道閃電之後，孩子們在一片漆黑之中驚恐地抱成了一團。幾顆大雨點啪噠啪噠地落到了樹葉上。

"快，弟兄們，快到帳篷裏去！"湯姆大聲喊。

孩子們拔腿就跑，在黑暗中跌跌撞撞，常被腳下的樹根老藤絆倒，沒有兩個孩子是往一個方向跑的。一陣兇猛的狂風呼嘯着掠過樹林，把所有的東西都吹得叫了起來。眩目的閃電一道緊跟着一道，震耳欲聾的雷聲一陣接着一陣。那時一陣傾盆大雨潑了下來，越颳越猛的颶風把雨順着地面颳成一片片雨幕。孩子們互相叫喊着，但是他們的叫喊聲完全被呼嘯的狂風和隆隆的雷聲淹沒了。不過，最後他們還是一個個湧進了露營的地方，躲到了帳篷底下，又冷，又怕，個個都成了落湯雞。

(美) 馬克·吐溫：《湯姆·索耶歷險記》

51　The Sky Was Dark and Lowering

It had been gradually getting overcast, and now the sky was dark and lowering, save where the glory of the departing sun piled up masses[1] of gold and burning fire, decaying embers of which gleamed here and there through the black veil, and shone redly down upon the earth. The wind began to moan in hollow murmurs[2], as the sun went down carrying glad day elsewhere; and a train of dull clouds coming up against it[3], menaced thunder and lightning. Large drops of rain soon began to fall, and, as the storm clouds came sailing onward, others supplied the void they left behind[4] and spread over all the sky. Then was heard the low rumbling of distant thunder, then the lightning quivered, and then the darkness of an hour seemed to have gathered in an instant.

Charles Dickens: The Old Curiosity Shop

---

1. masses：原義 "塊" 、 "團" ，這裏喻指雲團。
2. hollow murmurs：空洞低沉的聲音。
3. against it：此處的 "it" 指前面一句的 "black veil" ， "against it" ：以黑暗的天空為背景；在黑暗的天空的映襯下。

五十一　天幕低垂

　　天色漸漸變得陰沉，這會兒，天空開始暗了下來，天幕低垂。只有夕陽的餘輝，堆成金色和火紅的雲簇，這裏那裏閃爍着行將熄滅的餘火，透過黑幕，在大地上投下紅艷的色彩。太陽一落，帶走了白晝的歡樂，晚風開始嗚嗚地悲鳴。團團烏雲結集天空，電閃雷鳴迫在眉睫。大滴大滴的雨很快落了下來，攜有暴風雨的濃雲向前飄過去，其他的濃雲隨即滾滾而至，傾刻佈滿了整個天空。接着，便聽見遠處低沉的隆隆雷聲，之後電光閃動，霎時間就變得天昏地暗起來。

　　　　　　　　　　　　　　　(英) 狄更斯：《老古玩店》

---

4. others supplied the void they left behind：其他的雲補上它們（指之前的雲）所遺留的空隙。

52 Torrents

The morning came. The sky, which had been remarkably clear down to within a day or two, was overcast, and the weather threatening, the wind having an unmistakable hint of water in it. Henchard wished he had not been quite so sure about the continuance of a fair season. But it was too late to modify or postpone, and the proceedings went on. At twelve o'clock the rain began to fall, small and steady, commencing and increasing so insensibly that it was difficult to state exactly when dry weather ended or wet established itself. In an hour the slight moisture resolved itself into a monotonous smiting of earth by heaven, in torrents to which no end could be prognosticated.

A number of people had heroically gathered in the field, but by three o'clock Henchard discerned that his project was doomed to end in failure. The hams at the top of the poles dripped watered smoke in the form of a brown liquor, the pig shivered in the wind, the grain of the deal tables showed through the sticking table-cloths, for the awning allowed the rain to drift under at its will, and to enclose the sides at this

五十二　傾盆大雨

那天早晨，一直到最近一兩天還非常明淨的天空佈滿了陰雲，那樣子十分嚇人。風明顯地預示着雨要來了。亨查德但願他沒有那麼拿得穩，以為天氣會一直好下去。但是，要想法補救，或者延期，時間都已經來不及了，一切還是照常進行。十二點鐘開始下雨，雨雖然小，可是持續不斷，雨從開始下，到越來越凶，簡直分不出何時開始下雨。不到一小時，濛濛細雨變成了傾盆大雨，像上天一個勁兒地敲打着地面，真沒法預料這場雨何時才會收場。

有幾個人勇敢地聚集在這塊田上，但是，到了三點鐘的時候，亨查德看去，他的計劃注定要失敗了。杆頭上的火腿，往下滴着煙黃色的水珠，豬在風裏打哆嗦，那幾張做買賣用的桌子因為桌布濕透了，露出了木紋來。遮蓬已經檔不住雨，雨水就任意流淌了下來。而在這個時候，再

hour seemed a useless undertaking. The landscape over the river disappeared; the wind played on the tent-cords in Æolian[1] improvisations; and at length rose to such a pitch that the whole erection slanted to the ground, those who had taken shelter within it having to crawl out on their hands and knees.

Thomas Hardy: <u>The Mayor of Casterbridge</u>

---

1. Æolian：風神 Æolus 的，也是一種音樂模式。這裏，"the wind play...in Æolian improvisations" 是一種音樂意象，風吹着帳篷繩索，像即興彈撥風神的豎琴，嘯嘯作響。

把四邊遮起來，似乎也不會有甚麼作用了。河上的景色不
見了；風在大發神威，吹颳着帳篷的繩索；最後一陣狂風
竟然把整個帳篷颳倒在地，原在裏面躲雨的一些人只好四
條腿爬出來。

（英）哈代：《卡斯特橋市長》

53   A Cleft between Snowdrifts

The sky was brilliantly blue, and the sunlight on the glittering white stretches of prairie[1] was almost blinding. As Ántonia said, the whole world was changed by the snow; we kept looking in vain for familiar landmarks. The deep arroyo[2] through which Squaw[3] Creek wound was now only a cleft between snowdrifts — very blue when one looked down into it. The tree-tops that had been gold all the autumn were dwarfed and twisted, as if they would never have any life in them again. The few little cedars which were so dull and dingy before, now stood out a strong, dusky green. The wind had the burning taste of fresh snow; my throat and nostrils smarted as if someone had opened a hartshorn bottle. The cold stung, and at the same time delighted one. My horse's breath rose like steam, and whenever we stopped he smoked all over. The cornfields got back a little of their colour[4] under the dazzling light, and stood the palest possible gold in the

---

1. white stretches of prairie：一片白茫茫的大草原，這裏的 white 指 snow。
2. arroyo：（美國用語）小河，小溪，旱谷。

五十三　草原雪景

　　天空藍得耀眼，陽光照射在白茫茫的大草原上，發出眩目的閃光。正如安東尼亞所說，雪讓整個世界都變了樣。我們一直在尋找着熟悉的界標，卻總是白費心機。印女溪蜿蜒流過的那條深深的溪谷，如今只是雪堆中的一條裂縫——朝下望去，溪水湛藍湛藍的。整個秋天一直金光燦燦的樹梢，現在被壓得歪七扭八的，變矮了，彷彿不會再有甚麼生命了。那幾棵小雪松，以前暗淡無光，沒有生氣。如今挺立在雪堆之中，顯得強勁翠綠，引人注目。風夾帶着一種新鮮雪的灼人味兒，我的喉嚨和鼻子感到一陣刺痛，好像有人打開了一個氨水瓶。寒氣刺骨，卻又讓人覺得振奮，我的馬兒呼出的鼻息像水蒸汽似地向上升騰，我們一停下來，它便渾身冒熱氣。在耀眼的陽光下，玉米地稍稍恢復了點它們的元氣，在陽光和白雪中泛着淡淡的

---

3. Squaw：美洲印第安女人

4. got back a little of their colour：colour 既可解 "色彩"，也可指 "元氣"，是語帶相關的修辭手法。

sun and snow. All about us the snow was crusted in shallow
terraces with tracings like ripple-marks at the edges, curly
waves that were the actual impression of the stinging lash in
the wind.

Willa Cather: <u>My Ántonia</u>

金黃色。我們周圍的雪結成了一層層薄薄的雪殼,邊緣帶
有像是沙上的浪痕。這些彎彎曲曲的波紋,是狂風襲擊留
下的確切的印記。

（美）薇拉・凱瑟：《我的安東尼亞》

54   The Flakes

The flakes fell fast and thick, soon covering the ground some inches deep, and spreading abroad a solemn stillness. The rolling wheels were noiseless; and the sharp ring and clatter of the horses' hoofs, became a dull, muffled tramp. The life of their progress seemed to be slowly hushed, and something death-like to usurp its place[1].

Shading his eyes from the falling snow, which froze upon their lashes and obscured his sight, Kit often tried to catch the earliest glimpse of twinkling lights denoting their approach to some not distant town. He could descry objects enough at such times, but none correctly. Now a tall church spire appeared in view, which presently became a tree, a barn, a shadow on the ground, thrown on it by their own bright lamps. Now there were horsemen, foot-passengers, carriages,

---

1. The life of their progress ... usurp its place：這兩句寫得十分奧妙，修辭也很有特色。"他們前進的生命"是一語雙關，既指行駛中的馬車，也指坐在車裏隨車前進的人；"漸漸地窒息。"則是一種擬人化的手法，把馬車喻為一個生命體，在黑夜雪中行走，被紛紛大雪漸漸蒙着了窒息了，最後變成"死一般的沉寂"。

五十四　雪花

　　片片雪花落得又急又密，很快便在地上積起幾吋厚，給大地籠罩上一層蕭穆的寂靜。滾滾的車輪已悄然無聲，尖銳的鈴聲和馬蹄的得得聲變成了呆滯而壓抑了的踐踏聲。他們前進的生命彷彿漸漸地窒息，代之以死一般的沉寂。

　　凱特掩着眼擋住雪花，不讓雪花在睫毛凝結遮住視綫。他常常希望早些看到閃爍的燈光，標示他們不遠處就可到達某個城市了。在這種時候他也能夠辨認出一些事物，但甚麼也看不真切。這會兒眼前出現了一座高高的教堂的尖頂，一經他們明亮的燈光照射，即時變成地上的一棵樹、一座穀倉，一個影子。現在有騎馬的人、步行的

going on before, or meeting them in narrow ways; which, when they were close upon them, turned to shadows too. A wall, a ruin, a sturdy gable-end, would rise up in the road; and when they were plunging headlong at it, would be the road itself. Strange turnings too, bridges, and sheets of water, appeared to start up here and there, making the way doubtful and uncertain; and yet they were on the same bare road, and these things, like the others, as they were passed, turned into dim illusions[2].

Charles Dickens: <u>The Old Curiosity Shop</u>

---

2. dim illusions：是這一大段描寫的畫龍點睛之筆，指夜晚坐在馬車裏透過大雪觀景的感受。雪花給一切人和物都塗上了一層朦朧的色彩。透過路燈和馬車燈光，種種景象都好像海市蜃樓，變成一個個"朦朧的幻象"。

人、車輛在前面移動，或者在狹窄的街道上跟他們迎面相逢；但是，他們一經來到身邊，也即時變成了影子。道路中心也常會突然閃出一堵牆、一片廢墟、一個堅實的山牆屋頂；可是，當他們迎面撞上去時，卻依然是空空的道路本身。還有奇怪的拐彎處、橋樑和片片積水，好像時時突然出現，使道路變得疑竇叢生，模糊不清；但是，他們還是在同一條光溜溜的大路上。這些事物跟其他事物一樣，等他們走過時又立即變成了朦朧的幻象。

(英) 狄更斯：《老古玩店》

159

55　The Comet of the Year 1812

It was clear and frosty. Above the dirty, ill-lit streets, above the black roofs, stretched the dark, starry sky. Only as he gazed up at the sky did Pierre feel the humiliating pettiness of all earthly things compared with the heights to which his soul had just been raised. At the entrance to the Arbat Square an immense expanse of dark, starry sky appeared before his eyes. Almost in the center of it, above the Prechistensky Boulevard, surrounded and spangled on all sides by stars, but distinct from them by its nearness to the earth, with its white light and its long upturned tail, shone the huge, brilliant comet of the year 1812 — the comet that was said to portend all kinds of horrors and the end of the world. In Pierre, however, that bright star with its long, luminous tail aroused no feeling of dread. On the contrary, he gazed joyously, his eyes moist with tears, at that radiant star which, having traveled in its orbit with inconceivable velocity through

五十五　一八一二年的彗星

　　天氣冰冷，天色明淨。在污穢，昏暗的街道上，在黑色的屋頂上，是一片黑魆魆的星空。皮埃爾只有在仰望着夜空時感到，跟他的心靈剛才達到的高度相比，塵世間的一切又是多麼卑微。到達阿伯特廣場時，展現在他眼前的是一片空曠，幽暗的星空。就在伯來契斯頓斯卡大道上方的這片星空的中心，一顆巨大的，燦爛的一八一二年的彗星在閃耀着，它的四周有無數星辰簇擁着它。但它和別的星星不同，它最接近地面，射出白光，而且有一條長長的向上翹起的尾巴。據說這顆彗星預示着世上一切恐怖的事件和世界末日的來臨。然而，那顆明亮的，拖着長長閃光的尾巴的彗星，並沒有在皮埃爾心中激起任何恐怖的感覺。恰恰相反，他用一雙濕潤的淚眼，以愉快的心情凝望着這顆燦爛的星辰。這顆彗星，沿着運行的軌道，以不可

infinite space, seemed suddenly, like an arrow piercing the earth, to remain fixed in its chosen spot in the black firmament, tail firmly poised, shining and disporting[1] itself with its white light amid countless other scintillating[2] stars.

Lev Tolstoy: <u>War and Peace</u>

---

1. disporting：以……自娛，嬉戲。
2. scintillating：閃爍光亮的。

思議的速度飛越無限的宇宙。忽然間，彷彿一支射入地球的箭，插在黑暗的夜空中它所選定的位置，尾巴穩穩地懸在那裏，閃爍着白光，在其他無數閃耀着光芒的星星之間嬉戲。

（俄）列夫·托爾斯泰：《戰爭與和平》

Landscapes
地貌

56　The Road to Roncevaux

The bus climbed steadily up the road. The country was barren and rocks stuck up through the clay. There was no grass beside the road. Looking back we could see the country spread out below. Far back the fields were squares of green and brown on the hillsides. Making the horizon[1] were the brown mountains. They were strangely shaped. As we climbed higher the horizon kept changing. As the bus ground slowly up the road we could see other mountains coming up in the south. Then the road came over the crest, flattened out, and went into a forest. It was a forest of cork oaks, and the sun came through the trees in patches, and there were cattle grazing back in the trees. We went through the forest and the road came out and turned along a rise of land, and out ahead of us was a rolling green plain, with dark mountains beyond it. These were not like the brown, heat-baked mountains we had left behind. These were wooded and there were clouds coming down from them. The green plain

---

1. horizon：原義 "地平綫"，這裏指眼前的山勢輪廓，視綫所及的景象。

五十六　越山之路

　　汽車沿着公路不斷地往上攀登，山上一片荒涼貧瘠，
塊塊巖石裸露突現在泥地上，路邊寸草不見。回頭看，綿
延的原野展現在眼前，可以看到遠處山坡上一塊塊方形的
綠色和棕色的田野，褐色的羣山與天際相接。這些山的山
形都很奇特，每登高一步，羣山的輪廓不斷地改變。隨着
汽車沿公路緩緩攀登，我們看到南面又有新的山巒出現。
接着公路越過山頂，漸漸轉為平坦，進入了一片樹林，那
是一片軟木橡木林，陽光透過枝葉斑斑駁駁地射進林地。
牛羣在樹林深處啃吃青草。我們的車子穿過樹林，在一塊
高崗處拐彎。面前是一塊起伏的綠色平原，再往前，是黛
色的羣山，跟那些落在我們後面的烤焦了的褐色山巒不
同。山上林木繁茂，林間雲霧繚繞。綠色的原野朝前方伸

stretched off. It was cut by fences and the white of the road showed through the trunks of a double line of trees that crossed the plain toward the north. As we came to the edge of the rise we saw the red roofs and white houses of Burguete ahead strung out on the plain, and away off on the shoulder of the first dark mountain was the gray metal-sheathed roof of the monastery of Roncesvalles.

"There's Roncevaux[2]," I said.

Ernest Hemingway: <u>The Sun Also Rises</u>

---

2. Roncevaux：隆塞沃，法語名字，地處比利牛斯山脈（Pyrenees）南麓一山隘邊，在潘普洛納東北。

展開去，被籬笆隔成一塊塊。在一排雙行樹中間，一條白色大道穿越平原向北而去。當車子駛到高崗的邊緣，我們看到前面平原上伯爾蓋特一排排的白房子和紅屋頂。在遠處第一座黛色山崗的山肩上，閃現出隆塞斯凡爾斯修道院的金屬包蓋的灰色屋頂。

"那裏就是隆塞沃了，"我說。

(美) 海明威：《太陽照常升起》

57　The Austrians' Mountains

Beyond the mule train the road was empty and we climbed through the hills and then went down over the shoulder[1] of a long hill into a river-valley. There were trees along both sides of the road and through the right line of trees I saw the river, the water clear, fast and shallow. The river was low and there were stretches of sand and pebbles with a narrow channel of water and sometimes the water spread like a sheen over the pebbly bed. Close to the bank I saw deep pools, the water blue like the sky. I saw arched stone bridges over the river where tracks turned off from the road and we passed stone farmhouses with pear trees candelabraed[2] against their south walls and low stone walls in the fields. The road went up the valley a long way and then we turned off and commenced to climb into the hills again. The road climbed steeply going up and back and forth through chestnut woods to level finally along a ridge. I could look down through the woods and see, far below, with the

---

1. shoulder：地理名詞，山肩，谷肩
2. candelabraed：candelabra 原義 "燭台"，"火台"，這裏用作動詞，意為點綴。

五十七　奧地利雪山

　　越過騾子的隊伍，路就空了。我們翻過幾座小山後，便沿着一條長長的山肩走進了一個河谷。路的兩旁都是樹，從右邊的樹隙間可以望見一條河，河水淺淺的，清澈見底，流得很快。河牀很淺，有些河段看得見泥沙和圓石子，中間只有窄窄的一點水流。有時水流過河牀上的卵石，好像是一層鋪開的發光體。近岸邊，我看見有些深深的水潭，潭水碧藍像天色。我看到河面上有數座弓形的石橋，在那裏，一些小徑從大路叉了開去。我們經過了一些農夫的石屋子，南面的牆邊和農田裏矮矮的石牆上都有梨樹點綴其間。我們沿着上山谷的路走了很遠，拐個彎再開始往上爬。山路漸漸陡峭，盤來繞去，穿過栗子樹林，最後來到山脊上一處較為平坦的地方。從樹林間，看得見遠

sun on it, the line of the river that separated the two armies. We went along the rough new military road that followed the crest of the ridge and I looked to the north at the two ranges of mountains, green and dark to the snow-line and then white and lovely in the sun. Then, as the road mounted along the ridge, I saw a third range of mountains, higher snow mountains, that looked chalky white and furrowed, with strange planes, and then there were mountains far off beyond all these that you could hardly tell if you really saw. Those were all the Austrians' mountains and we had nothing like them. Ahead there was a rounded turn-off in the road to the right and looking down I could see the road dropping through the trees.

Ernest Hemingway: <u>A Farewell to Arms</u>

處下面太陽照耀下，河流宛如一條細綫，這條河把兩軍隔開。我們沿山頂在一條新修的凹凸不平的軍用小道上走着。往北看，只見有二排大山，近雪綫處呈現暗綠色，雪綫以上，一片白晃晃的，在陽光下煞是可愛。沿山脊再往上爬，我看見第三排山脈，更高的雪山，山頂的積雪如有皺紋的白堊，呈現出各種奇特的平面。這排山後還有山，因為相距極遠，説不清是真山還是假山。那些都是奧地利的高山峻嶺，我們這邊沒有那樣的大山。往前走，路邊有個圓形的拐彎處，從那裏看得見路在樹林間往下滑。

(美) 海明威：《永別了，武器》

58 McDougal's Cave

The mouth of the cave was up the hillside — an opening shaped like a letter A. Its massive oaken door stood unbarred. Within was a small chamber, chilly as an icehouse, and walled by nature with solid limestone that was dewy with a cold sweat. It was romantic and mysterious to stand here in the deep gloom and look out upon the green valley shining in the sun.

...

By and by the procession went filing down the steep descent of the main avenue, the flickering rank of lights dimly revealing the lofty walls of rock almost to their point of junction sixty feet overhead. This main avenue was not more than eight or ten feet wide. Every few steps other lofty and still narrower crevices branched from it on either hand — for McDougal's Cave was but a vast labyrinth[1] of crooked aisles that ran into each other and out again and led nowhere.

---

1. labyrinth：迷宮，曲徑。

五十八　麥克道格爾大山洞

　　山洞的口在半山腰上——進口的地方像個Ａ字形。那扇笨重的橡木大門並沒有閂上，裏面有個小石室，冷得像冰窖。四周是天然形成的堅硬的石灰石牆壁，那上面像是出冷汗似地冒着水珠。在這裏，站在深沉的陰暗中，往外瞧那陽光下閃閃發光的青翠山谷，給人一種浪漫的神秘感……

　　漸漸大家排成縱列順着主要通道的陡坡一個一個往下走，那一行閃爍不定的燭光模模糊糊地照出了高聳的石壁，幾乎照到頭頂上六十呎高處兩壁相接的地方。這條主要通道不過八到十呎寬，每隔幾步就有其他高聳、更窄的裂縫從這條大道兩旁叉開去——因為麥克道格爾洞原是由許許多多其他彎彎曲曲的小通道組成的一個龐大迷宮。那些小通道互相交叉，又互相分開，不知究竟通到甚麼地

It was said that one might wander days and nights together through its intricate tangle of rifts[2] and chasms[3], and never find the end of the cave; and that he might go down and down, and still down, into the earth, and it was just the same — labyrinth underneath labyrinth, and no end to any of them. No man "knew" the cave. That was an impossible thing. Most of the young men knew a portion of it, and it was not customary to venture much beyond this known portion. Tom Sawyer knew as much of the cave as anyone.

Mark Twain: The Adventures of Tom Sawyer

---

2. rifts：裂縫，空隙。
3. chasms：裂口，深淵。

方。據說遊洞的人可以在那些錯綜複雜的裂縫和巖口裏隨便走，走上幾天幾夜，也始終找不到洞的盡頭；他儘可以老往下走，往下走，走了又走，一直往地底下鑽，其結果也一樣——迷宮之下還是迷宮，哪一個也走不到底。若說誰也不熟悉這個大山洞，是不可能的。但大部分的年輕男子只熟悉洞的一部分，而且照例都不敢超越出他們所熟悉的這一部分；湯姆對這個洞所知道的也不比別人多。

(美) 馬克・吐溫：《湯姆・索耶歷險記》

59   The Happy Valley

We stood on a slope of a wooded hill, and the path wound away before us to a valley, by the side of a running stream. There were no dark trees here, no tangled undergrowth, but on either side of the narrow path stood azaleas and rhododendrons, not blood-coloured like the giants in the drive, but salmon, white, and gold, things of beauty and of grace, drooping their lovely, delicate heads in the soft summer rain.

The air was full of their scent, sweet and heady, and it seemed to me as though their very essence had mingled with the running waters of the stream, and become one with the falling rain and the dank rich moss beneath our feet. There was no sound here but the tumbling of the little stream, and the quiet rain. When Maxim spoke, his voice was hushed too, gentle and low, as if he had no wish to break upon the silence.

"We call it the Happy Valley," he said.

We stood quite still, not speaking, looking down upon the clear white faces of the flowers closest to us, and Maxim stooped, and picked up a fallen petal and gave it to me. It was crushed and bruised, and turning brown at the curled edge, but as I rubbed it across my hand the scent rose to me, sweet and strong, vivid as the living tree from which it came.

五十九 快活谷

我們站在樹木遍佈的小山坡上，眼前的小徑蜿蜒至一座山谷，一直通到一條潺潺的溪流邊。這裏沒有幽暗的大樹，也沒有錯綜的灌木叢。狹窄的小徑兩旁開滿了杜鵑花和石楠，顏色不像車道上的巨型花朵那樣呈血紅色。這裏的花兒有的呈橙色，有的呈白色和金黃色，顯得美麗而優雅。在夏季的微雨中，都垂着它們那婀娜嬌柔的花冠。

空氣中洋溢着花香，甜美得薰人欲醉，我們彷彿覺得鮮花的芬芳已經融進了山溪的流水之中，已經和落下的雨點、腳下濕漉漉的茂密的苔蘚融成了一體。這兒除了溪流的淙淙聲和恬靜的細雨聲，再也聽不見別的聲音。馬克西姆說話時把嗓音壓得低低的，柔聲細語，像是不想打擾四下的寧靜。

"我們把它叫做快活谷，"他這麼跟我說。

我們默不作聲地站着，觀賞着靠近我們周圍的那些花兒潔白的臉龐。馬克西姆彎下腰去，拾起一片落在地上的花瓣，把它遞給了我。花瓣已被壓碎碰損，捲曲的邊沿已經變成褐色。可是，當我把它放在手裏揉搓時，依然聞到一股花香，跟長在活樹上的花兒的香味一樣的濃烈甜美。

Then the birds began. First a blackbird, his note clear and cool above the running stream, and after a moment he had answer from his fellow hidden in the woods behind us, and soon the still air about us was made turbulent with song, pursuing us as we wandered down into the valley, and the fragrance of the white petals followed us too. It was disturbing[1], like an enchanted place. I had not thought it could be as beautiful as this.

The sky, now overcast and sullen, so changed from the early afternoon, and the steady insistent rain could not disturb the soft quietude of the valley; the rain and the rivulet mingled with one another, and the liquid note of the black-bird fell upon the damp air in harmony with them both. I brushed the dripping heads of azaleas as I passed, so close they grew together, bordering the path. Little drops of water fell onto my hands from the soaked petals. There were petals at my feet too, brown and sodden, bearing their scent upon them still, and a richer, older scent as well, the smell of deep moss and bitter earth, the stems of bracken, and the twisted buried roots of trees.

Daphne du Maurier: Rebecca

---

1. disturbing：原義為 "擾亂，攪動"，常指惱人的事；這裏用以描述美麗如仙境的景色，給人帶來意外激動的心境。

接着，鳥兒開始啁啾。起初是一隻畫眉，牠的歌聲清脆爽朗，在汩汩的小溪上方飄蕩。不一會兒，藏在我們身後樹林中的鳥兒發出了回答聲，四下的沉寂頓時化作一片嘈雜的鳥語聲。鳥兒的歌聲尾隨着我們漫遊進山谷，白色花瓣的芬芳也一直陪伴着我們。這裏簡直像個魔境，讓人心馳神移，我未曾料到這一切竟會是如此之美。

　　天空這會兒烏雲密佈，開始陰沉起來，跟午後剛開始時的晴朗大不相同。瑟瑟細雨下個不停，卻絲毫不驚擾山谷的靜謐。雨聲和溪流聲已經相互交融。畫眉鳥清澈的歌聲在潮濕的空中迴蕩，與細雨聲和溪水聲相映成趣。杜鵑花沿着小徑成簇成簇地長在一起，我一路走過，身子擦過它們那滴着水的花冠。小水滴從浸飽了水份的花瓣滴到我的手上。我的腳邊也有許多花瓣，浸透了水份，顏色開始發黃，可是芳香猶存，而且還間雜着茂密的苔蘚的清香和泥土的苦澀味，還有蕨類的莖根和盤曲入地的樹根的氣味，都是一些更馥郁更古舊的氣息。

　　　　　　　　(英) 達夫妮·杜莫里埃：《蝴蝶夢》

60 Not Earthly Music

I came into the valley, as the evening sun was shining
on the remote heights of snow, that closed it in, like eternal
clouds. The bases of the mountains forming the gorge in
which the little village lay, were richly green, and high above
this gentler vegetation, grew forests of dark fir, cleaving the
wintry snow-drift, wedge-like, and stemming the avalanche.
Above these, were range upon range of craggy steeps, grey
rock, bright ice, and smooth verdure-specks[1] of pasture, all
gradually blending with the crowning snow. Dotted here and
there on the mountain-sides, each tiny dot a home, were lonely
wooden cottages, so dwarfed by[2] the towering heights[3] that
they appeared too small for toys. So did even the clustered
village in the valley, with its wooden bridge across the stream,
where the stream tumbled over broken rocks, and roared away
among the trees. In the quiet air, there was a sound of distant
singing — shepherd voices; but, as one bright evening cloud

---

1. verdure-specks：點點青翠的樣子。
2. dwarfed by：使……變得矮小。（dwarf = 侏儒）
3. towering heights：指高聳的山或建築物。

六十　並非人間的音樂

　　我走進山谷裏面，夕陽的餘暉正照在遠處的雪山上。
那些雪山把山谷團團圍起，好似恆久不變的白雲，這個小
山村座落在這些山腳下的峽谷裏。峽谷青翠葱鬱，在這片
柔綠的上方為一片茂密的樅樹林帶，像楔子似地把冬日的
雪堆截斷，堵住了雪崩。林木上面，一層又一層的危崖峭
壁、蒼巖灰石、耀眼眩目的冰塊，和疏落平緩的青草地，
交替疊累而上，漸漸和山頂的白雪融為一體。山坡上，這
兒那兒有些孤零的小板屋，每一板屋都只是一星一點，但
卻又是一家一戶，從高入雲霄的山上望去，顯得比玩具房
子還小。那些羣集在谷底上的小村落，情況也大抵如此。
村落裏有座木橋，橫跨山澗，溪流就在亂石上飛濺而過，
在樹林裏呼嘯而去。在寧靜的大氣中，傳來遠處的歌聲
──牧羊人的歌聲；但恰好那時，山腰飄來一朵明麗的晚

floated midway along the mountain-side, I could almost have believed it came from there, and was not earthly music. All at once, in this serenity, great Nature spoke to me; and soothed me to lay down my weary head upon the grass.

Charles Dickens: <u>David Copperfield</u>

霞，我幾乎以為那歌聲是從那朵晚霞中飄蕩出來的，並非人間的音樂。在這樣的靜謐之中，偉大的大自然突然向我說話了，它撫慰着我使我把疲乏的頭枕在草地上。

(英) 狄更斯：《大衛·科波菲爾》

61　Glens Shut In by Hills

I left him there, and proceeded down the valley alone. The grey church looked greyer, and the lonely churchyard lonelier. I distinguished a moor sheep cropping the short turf on the graves. It was sweet, warm weather — too warm for travelling; but the heat did not hinder me from enjoying the delightful scenery above and below; had I seen it nearer August, I'm sure it would have tempted me to waste a month among its solitudes. In winter, nothing more dreary, in summer, nothing more divine, than those glens shut in by hills, and those bluff, bold swells[1] of heath.

Emily Brontë: Wuthering Heights

1.　swells：原義 "隆起的"，這裏轉義圓形的小山丘。

六十一 羣山遮掩的幽谷

我讓僕人留在那裏，自己一個人進了山谷。那灰色的教堂越發顯得灰暗，教堂外面的墳地也顯得越發孤寂。我看清楚一隻野羊正在墳頭上啃吃草皮。天氣很好，很暖和——對旅行者來説又稍嫌熱了點，卻並不影響我的遊興，我還是相當盡情地飽覽着山上山下的美景。若是在臨近八月天見到這樣的景色，我敢説它會誘我在這個靜謐的地方耗上一個月的時間。那些羣山遮掩的幽谷、石楠叢生的峭壁和山丘，在冬天沒有甚麼地方比它們更荒涼，可是，在夏天卻又是最美妙不過的了。

(英) 艾米利‧勃朗特：《呼嘯山莊》

62　The Glen Wound to Their Very Core

The breeze was from the west: it came over the hills, sweet with scents of heath and rush; the sky was of stainless blue; the stream descending the ravine, swelled with past spring rains, poured along plentiful and clear, catching golden gleams from the sun, and sapphire tints from the firmament[1]. As we advanced and left the track, we trod a soft turf, mossy fine and emerald green, minutely enamelled[2] with a tiny white flower, and spangled with a star-like yellow blossom: the hills, meantime, shut us quite in; for the glen, towards its head, wound to their very core.

Charlotte Brontë: Jane Eyre

1.　firmament：文學用語，指天空。
2.　enamelled：像上了光漆的。

六十二　幽谷盡頭

　　微風來自西邊，它帶着石楠和燈芯草的芬芳吹過小山。天空碧澄，沒有一絲雲彩；溪水順着幽谷流淌下去，幾場春雨使水位上漲，流水清澈，盈盈瀉下，水面泛着太陽的粼粼金光，映着穹蒼的藍寶石色澤。我們往前走着，離開了小徑，踏上了柔軟草地。草細得像苔蘚，綠得像翡翠。草地上精緻地點綴着一朵朵小白花，還閃爍着一些星星點點的小黃花。這時候我們已置身於重重山巒的包圍之中；因為幽谷已經到了盡頭，蜿蜒到了羣山的中央。

　　　　　　　　　(英) 夏洛特・勃朗特：《簡・愛》

63   The Delicious Vale

At the end of this march I came to an opening, where the country seemed to descend to the west, and a little spring of fresh water, which issued out of the side of the hill by me, run the other way, that is, due east; and the country appeared so fresh, so green, so flourishing, everything being in a constant verdure, or flourish of spring, that it looked like a planted garden.

I descended a little on the side of that delicious vale[1], surveying it with a secret kind of pleasure (though mixed with my other afflicting thoughts), to think that this was all my own, that I was king and lord of all this country indefeasibly and had a right of possession; and if I could convey it, I might have it in inheritance, as completely as any lord of a manor in England. I saw here abundance of cocoa trees, orange and lemon and citron trees; but all wild and very few bearing any fruit, at least not then. However, the green limes that I gathered were not only pleasant to eat but very wholesome; and I mixed their juice afterwards with water, which made it very wholesome and very cool and refreshing.

Daniel Defoe: Robinson Crusoe

六十三　荒島上的世外桃源

　　我走到盡頭的時候，忽然來到一處開闊地，那裏的地勢彷彿向西傾斜，一股小小的清泉從我身旁的小山上溢出，朝另一方向，也就是正東的方向流去。這裏草木繁茂，清翠葱蘢，滿眼碧油油的，一派春色，宛如一座人工修建的花園。

　　我順着這個風景秀麗的山谷往下走了一段路，心懷一種暗自的愉悦（雖然也滲雜着我的另外一點苦惱之情）眺望着它。我心中在想，這一切現在都屬於我了，我是這一大片土地無可爭辯的君主和國王，對它擁有所有權。如果可以轉讓的話，我還可以像任何一個英國的莊園主一樣，把它作為遺產轉讓給我的子孫後代。在這裏我看到有許多可可樹、桔子樹、檸檬樹、和枸櫞樹；但全都是野生的，也很少結果實，至少這時候如此。可是，我採集到的青檸，吃起來不但味美可口，而且營養豐富。後來我把它的汁液羼上水，喝起來，既滋補，又清涼，又提神。

（英）笛福：《魯濱遜飄流記》

---

1. vale：詩歌用語，溪谷。

64　The Mother-forest

Pearl had not found the hour pass wearisomely, while her mother sat talking with the clergyman. The great black forest — stern as it showed itself to those who brought the guilt and troubles of the world into its bosom — became the playmate of the lonely infant, as well as it knew how. Sombre as it was, it put on the kindest of its moods to welcome her. It offered her the partridge-berries, the growth of the preceding autumn, but ripening only in the spring, and now red as drops of blood upon the withered leaves. These Pearl gathered, and was pleased with their wild flavor. The small denizens of the wilderness hardly took pains to move out of her path. A partridge, indeed, with a brood of ten behind her, ran forward threateningly, but soon repented of her fierceness, and clucked to her young ones not to be afraid. A pigeon, alone on a low branch, allowed Pearl to come beneath, and uttered a sound as much of greeting as alarm. A squirrel, from the lofty depths of his domestic tree, chattered either in anger or merriment, — for a squirrel is such a choleric and humorous little personage that it is hard to distinguish between his moods, — so he chattered at the child, and flung down a nut upon her head. It was a last year's nut, and already gnawed by his sharp tooth. A fox, startled from his sleep by

六十四　森林母親

　　當她的母親與牧師坐着談話的時候，珠兒並不覺得時間難熬。這幽暗的大森林對那些把人間的罪惡和煩惱帶進它的胸膛裏來的人來説是可畏的，但卻成了這個孤獨幼兒的遊伴。大森林看似陰沉，對她卻是以最最友善的態度表示歡迎。它將鷓鴣草莓獻給她，那是去年秋天長出，到今年春天結下的果實，這時一個個血紅的掛在樹枝上。珠兒很喜歡它的野味，採擷了許多。一些林中小動物，幾乎都不肯勞駕給她讓路，真的，有一隻鷓鴣，率着身後十隻小鷓鴣，氣勢洶洶地朝她衝了過來，但很快又為自己的莽撞而後悔，咯咯地呼喚牠的小雛，叫牠們不要害怕。一隻小鴿子，獨自停息在低低的樹枝上，在珠兒從牠下邊走過時，發出一種像是致敬，又像是驚恐的聲音。一隻高棲於樹頂的松鼠，嘰嘰喳喳叫個不停，不知是因為大發雷霆呢還是心花怒放──因為松鼠是這麼一種性情暴燥而滑稽的小動物，牠的脾性很難捉摸。牠一面對這個小女孩嘮叨不停，一面將一隻堅果扔到她頭上。那是去年結的果實，已經被牠的利齒啃咬過了。一隻狐狸，被她輕輕踩在落葉上

her light foot-step on the leaves, looked inquisitively at Pearl, as doubting whether it were better to steal off, or renew his nap on the same spot. A wolf, it is said, — but here the tale has surely lapsed into the improbable, — came up, and smelt of Pearl's robe, and offered his savage head to be patted by her hand. The truth seems to be, however, that the mother-forest, and these wild things which it nourished, all recognized a kindred wildness in the human child.

Nathaniel Hawthorne: The Scarlet Letter

的腳步聲驚醒，好奇地打量着她，似乎拿不定主意倒底是溜之大吉呢還是呆在原處繼續打瞌睡。據說，有一隻狼──故事說到這裏，確實荒誕不經的了──走上前來，嗅嗅珠兒的衣服，抬起牠那兇殘的頭，想讓她拍拍。不過，實情可能是：森林母親和她所養育的野性動物，都從這個人類孩子的身上看到了跟牠們類似的野性來。

(美) 霍桑：《紅字》

65　A Glimpse of the Better Land

The week had gone round to the Saturday following that beating of my heart in the church; and every day had been so bright and blue, that to ramble in the woods, and to see the light striking down among the transparent[1] leaves, and sparkling in the beautiful interlacings[2] of the shadows of the trees, while the birds poured out their songs, and the air was drowsy with the hum of insects, had been most delightful. We had one favourite spot, deep in moss and last year's leaves, where there were some felled trees from which the bark was all stripped off. Seated among these, we looked through a green vista supported by thousands of natural columns, the whitened stems of trees, upon a distant prospect made so radiant by its contrast with the shade in which we sat, and made so precious[3] by the arched perspective through which we saw it, was like a glimpse of the better land.

Charles Dickens: Bleak House

---

1. transparent：原義 "透明的"，這裏指樹葉叢中能夠透過陽光的明亮的間隙。 transparent leaves 意為有陽光照射的明亮的葉子。
2. interlacings：相互交錯，這裏指樹葉陰影的相互重疊交錯。
3. precious：珍貴的，美麗的，漂亮的。

六十五　美麗的仙境

今天又是星期六，從我在教堂裏心怦怦跳那一天起，差不多已經過了一星期；天天都是晴朗無雲的好天氣，所以，到林中漫步，看着陽光透過樹葉間隙照射下來，在樹影婆娑中閃閃發光，同時，鳥兒們盡情高唱，四周充滿了睏人的蟲鳴，使人感到心曠神怡。有一處地方我們特別鍾愛，那裏遍地是苔蘚和去年的落葉，還有幾株砍倒的樹，樹皮都已經剝落。我們坐在其中，透過那片由千百根天然柱子，和泛着白色的樹幹支撐着的綠色樹廊，眺望着遠處的景色。那裏陽光燦爛，和我們坐着的這片蔭影形成強烈的對照；我們透過這個弓形的樹廊，見到遠處的景色分外優美，彷彿瞥見了一個美麗的仙境。

(英) 狄更斯：《荒涼山莊》

66   The Calm and Silence of the Woods

It was the cool gray dawn, and there was a delicious sense of repose and peace in the deep pervading calm and silence of the woods. Not a leaf stirred; not a sound obtruded upon great Nature's meditation. Beaded dewdrops stood upon the leaves and grasses. A white layer of ashes covered the fire, and a thin blue breath of smoke rose straight into the air. Joe and Huck still slept.

Now, far away in the woods a bird called; another answered; presently the hammering of a woodpecker was heard. Gradually the cool dim gray of the morning whitened, and as gradually sounds multiplied and life manifested itself. The marvel of Nature shaking off sleep and going to work unfolded itself to the musing boy. A little green worm came crawling over a dewy leaf, lifting two-thirds of his body into the air from time to time and "sniffing around," then proceeding again — for he was measuring, Tom said; and when the worm approached him, of its own accord, he sat as still as a stone, with his hopes rising and falling, by turns, as the creature still came toward him or seemed inclined to go elsewhere; and when at last it considered a painful moment with its curved body in the air and then came decisively down upon Tom's leg and began a journey over him, his whole

六十六　林中清晨

　　那是涼爽，灰暗的黎明時分，在樹林裏一片深沉的寂靜中，彌漫着一種甜蜜的安息與和平的氣氛。樹葉紋絲不動；沒有一點兒聲音打擾大自然的沉思。露珠兒還留在樹葉和小草上，火堆上蓋着一層白灰，一縷淡淡的青煙徑直升上天空，喬和哈克還在沉睡。

　　這會兒，樹林深處有一隻鳥兒叫了起來；另一隻發出了應答聲，隨即又聽到了啄木鳥的啄木聲。涼爽暗淡的早晨漸漸發白了，各種聲音漸漸多了起來，一切都顯得生機盎然了。大自然的奇景擺脱了睡意，開始活動，在這個正在沉思的孩子面前漸漸展開。一條小青蟲，在一片有露水的葉子上爬了過來，牠不時把三分之二的身子向空中抬起，向四周"聞聞"再接着往前爬——湯姆説，牠是在量尺寸哩。當這條蟲子自動爬近他身邊時，他像塊石頭一般一動不動地坐着。那蟲子一時像是要繼續爬過來，一時又像是要爬向別處去，他的希望也就一時高漲，一時低落。後來那條蟲子把彎曲的身體伸向空中，苦苦思索一會兒，決意要爬上湯姆的腿，在他身上到處旅行。那時，他簡直

heart was glad — for that meant that he was going to have a new suit of clothes — without the shadow of a doubt a gaudy piratical uniform. Now a procession of ants appeared from nowhere in particular, and went about their labors; one struggled manfully by with a dead spider five times as big as itself in its arms, and lugged it straight up a tree trunk. A brown-spotted ladybug climbed the dizzy height of a grass blade, and Tom bent down close to it and said, "Ladybug, ladybug, fly away home, your house is on fire, your children's alone," and she took wing and went off to see about it — which did not surprise the boy, for he knew of old[1] that this insect was credulous about conflagrations, and he had practiced upon its simplicity more than once. A tumblebug came next, heaving sturdily at its ball, and Tom touched the creature, to see it shut its legs against its body and pretend to be dead. The birds were fairly rioting by this time. A catbird, the northern mocker[2], lit in a tree over Tom's head, and trilled[3] out her imitations of her neighbors in a rapture of enjoyment; then a shrill jay swept down, a flash of blue flame, and stopped on a twig almost within the boy's reach, cocked his head to one side and eyed the strangers with a consuming curiosity[4],

---

1. of old：古時，往時；如："the heroes of old" 昔日的英雄。
2. mocker = mockingbird（嘲鶇）

高興得心花怒放——因為這就表明他將會得到一套新衣服——毫無疑問，那會是一套漂亮的海盜式制服。接着，也不知從哪兒爬出來一大隊螞蟻，開始了牠們的勞作。其中一隻螞蟻掙扎着勇敢地拖着一隻比牠大五倍的蜘蛛，硬要把牠拖上樹幹。一隻帶褐色斑點的瓢蟲，爬上了一片草葉的絕頂，湯姆低下頭去，靠得很近對牠説："瓢蟲，瓢蟲，快飛回家吧，你家着火了，你的孩子沒人管。"於是，牠便展翅飛了起來，回家去看倒底怎樣——這並不讓孩子感到驚訝，因為他早就聽説這種昆蟲對於火災好犯疑心，他對牠那簡單的頭腦已開過不止一次的玩笑了。隨後又來了一隻金龜子，拚命使勁地搬動牠那糞蛋。湯姆碰了一下這小東西，想看看牠把腿縮回身子裝死的樣子。這時，許多鳥兒嘰嘰喳喳，已經喧鬧得相當厲害了。有一隻貓鵲——一種北方的學舌鳥——停落在湯姆頭頂的樹枝上，用牠婉轉的歌喉，模仿着鄰近其他鳥兒的叫聲，以表達牠欣喜若狂的心情；接着，一隻樫鳥尖聲叫着飛了下來，像是一團藍色的火焰一閃而過，停落在一根小樹枝上，湯姆一伸手幾乎就能搆得着牠。小鳥把腦袋一歪，非

---

3. trill：鳥的囀鳴。

4. consuming curiosity：consume 原意"消耗"，這裏用來描繪好奇的程度，表示"極之好奇"。

a gray squirrel and a big fellow of the "fox" kind came scurrying along, sitting up at intervals to inspect and chatter at the boys, for the wild things had probably never seen a human being before and scarcely knew whether to be afraid or not. All nature was wide awake and stirring, now; long lances of sunlight pierced down through the dense foliage far and near, and a few butterflies came fluttering upon the scene.

Mark Twain: *The Adventures of Tom Sawyer*

常好奇地望着這些陌生客，一隻灰色的松鼠和一隻像狐狸的大家夥急匆匆地跑了過來，每隔一會兒就坐下來看看這幾個孩子，又嘰嘰叫上幾聲，因為這些野生小動物恐怕以前從未見過一個人，根本不知道是不是應該害怕。此刻，整個大自然已經完全甦醒，活動了起來。一道道陽光透過濃密的樹葉，在遠近各處投射下來，幾隻花蝴蝶應景而飛。

（美）馬克‧吐溫：《湯姆‧索耶歷險記》

67 Haggard Egdon

It was a spot which returned upon the memory of those who loved it with an aspect of peculiar and kindly congruity. Smiling champaigns of flowers and fruit hardly do this, for they are permanently harmonious only with an existence of better reputation[1] as to its issues than the present. Twilight[2] combined with the scenery of Egdon Heath to evolve a thing majestic without severity, impressive without showiness, emphatic in its admonitions, grand in its simplicity. The qualifications[3] which frequently invest the façade[4] of a prison with far more dignity than is found in the façade of a palace double its size lent to this heath a sublimity[5] in which spots renowned for beauty of the accepted kind are utterly wanting. Fair prospects wed happily with fair times; but alas; if times

---

1. existence of better reputation：較為體面的人生。事實上，"Smiling champaigns of..." 這一整句話是對上文結論式的開頭語所作的進一步闡釋。它告訴讀者愛敦荒原的不同尋常之處，一般花果繁茂的原野給人美好的印象，只能和 "美好的人生" 相提並論、相互配合。但愛敦荒原卻給人溫藹和諧的面貌。

2. Twilight：譯為 "黃昏"、"暮色" 自然是好，但加上 "蒼蒼" 兩字更為傳神，把這片荒原的蒼茫荒涼之意一覽無餘地展現了出來。

六十七　荒涼的愛敦

　　這個地方，能夠讓愛它的人回憶起來覺得有一種不同尋常，溫藹和諧的面貌。花果繁茂、風景的明媚的原野是很難做到這一點的，因為那種原野，只有遇到一種在結局上比現在要好的人生，才能永遠兩相協調。蒼蒼的暮色和愛敦荒原的景物，共同造出一種風光，堂皇而不嚴峻，感人而無粉飾，有深遠的告誡性，有渾厚的純樸味。牢獄的外貌常有一種遠比宮殿的外觀更威嚴的氣魄，而現在荒原上也就是有了兩倍於這種氣魄，是擁有世俗以美見稱的地方所欠缺的。明媚的景物配上美好的時光，自然圓滿；但

---

3. qualifications：原義 "描寫"、"形容"，這裏比喻監獄的外觀給人造成的印象，擁有的氣魄。

4. façade：（法語），建築物的正面。

5. lent to this heath a sublimity：賦與這荒原一種崇高的氣魄。

be not fair! Men have oftener suffered from the mockery of a place too smiling for their reason than from the oppression of surroundings oversadly tinged. Haggard Egdon appealed to[6] a subtler and scarcer instinct, to a more recently learnt emotion, than that which responds to the sort of beauty called charming and fair.

Thomas Hardy: The Return of the Native

---

6. appeal to：有感染力，或引人入勝，〞to〞後面常接人。這裏顯然 指〞people with a subtler and scarcer instinct...〞。

是，唉！倘若時光並不美好，那該怎麼辦呢？人有時感到不好受，多半是因為景物過於美好，反而受到嘲弄；很少是因為周圍環境過於蕭瑟，因而感到心情壓抑。能夠跟荒涼的愛敦意氣相投的，是那種比較細膩和比較稀有的本性，一種新近才發生的感情，而不是那種只認媚艷為美的性情。

(英)哈代：《還鄉》

68   The Streamlet

Thus conversing, they entered sufficiently deep into the
wood to secure themselves from the observation of any casual
passenger along the forest-track. Here they sat down on a
luxuriant heap of moss; which, at some epoch of the preceding
century, had been a gigantic pine, with its roots and trunk
in the darksome shade, and its head aloft in the upper
atmosphere. It was a little dell where they had seated
themselves, with a leaf-strewn bank rising gently on either
side, and a brook flowing through the midst, over a bed of
fallen and drowned leaves. The trees impending over it had
flung down great branches, from time to time, which choked
up the current, and compelled it to form eddies and black
depths[1] at some points; while, in its swifter and livelier
passages, there appeared a channel-way of pebbles, and
brown, sparkling sand. Letting the eyes follow along the
course of the stream, they could catch the reflected light from
its water, at some short distance within the forest, but soon
lost all traces of it amid the bewilderment of tree-trunks and

---

1. black depth：深水潭

六十八　山澗小溪

　　她們邊說邊走，進了森林深處，來到一處絕不會被任何偶爾沿山間小道過往的行人注意的地方。在那裏她們在一叢茂密的青苔上坐下來；這個地方，在上個世紀的某個時期曾經有一棵巨大的松樹，濃陰遮蓋着樹根和樹幹，樹頂參天聳立。她們坐着的地方是個小山谷，兩邊山坡緩緩而起，上面落葉繽紛，一條溪流貫穿其間，水流從落葉上面流淌而過。俯懸在河上的樹木，不時往河裏投下枯枝樹幹，阻遏了流水，使河流的某些地段，形成了一些旋渦和深潭；而在幾處流水暢快、疾速的河段，可見到河底的碎石和閃閃發光的褐色泥沙。視綫順着溪流望去，在樹林不遠處，可以見到波光粼粼的水面，但不久便消失在迷亂的

underbrush[2], and here and there a huge rock, covered over with gray lichens. All these giant trees and boulders of granite seemed intent on making a mystery of the course of this small brook; fearing, perhaps, that, with its never-ceasing loquacity[3], it should whisper tales out of the heart of the old forest whence it flowed, or mirror its revelations on the smooth surface of a pool. Continually, indeed, as it stole onward, the streamlet kept up a babble, kind, quiet, soothing, but melancholy, like the voice of a young child that was spending its infancy without playfulness, and knew not how to be merry among sad acquaintance and events of sombre hue.

Nathaniel Hawthorne: <u>The Scarlet Letter</u>

---

2. underbrush：= undergrowth，長在樹林下的矮樹叢。

3. loquacity：原義 "多嘴"，"饒舌"，這裏比喻潺潺不停的流水聲。

樹幹和樹叢中間。只見這裏那裏，有一些長滿灰色苔蘚的巨石，所有這些參天大樹和花崗石，彷彿有意要造成這條小河的神秘，或許是怕那喋喋不休從這古老森林流出的溪水，會道出森林心中的秘密；或者擔心，在某個潭水平靜的水面上，會映現出它的隱情。真的，當這條小溪悄悄向前流動時，不斷地發出潺潺聲，親切、寧靜、給人以安慰而又不乏憂傷之情，那聲音像是一個不知玩耍而虛度了幼兒時光的小孩，不知怎樣在愁悶的友人之間和憂鬱的事件當中自尋歡娛。

（美）霍桑：《紅字》

69　Singular Symphonies

To the east of Casterbridge lay moors and meadows through which much water flowed. The wanderer in this direction who should stand still for a few moments on a quiet night, might hear singular symphonies from these waters, as from a lampless orchestra, all playing in their sundry tones from near and far parts of the moor. At a hole in a rotten weir they executed a recitative; where a tributary brook fell over a stone breastwork they trilled cheerily; under an arch they performed a metallic cymballing; and at Durnover Hole they hissed. The spot at which their instrumentation[1] rose loudest was a place called Ten Hatches, whence during high springs there proceeded a very fugue[2] of sounds.

Thomas Hardy: The Mayor of Casterbridge

---

1. instrumentation：（音樂用語）樂器演奏法。這裏喻指流水聲像不同的樂器在合奏。

2. fugue：（音樂用語）賦格曲。這裏用來比喻發出各種層層疊疊聲響的水流聲。

六十九　超凡的交響樂

卡斯特橋的東面，是一片荒野和草地，上面有多量的水流。到這裏來閒逛的人，若是在寂靜的夜晚靜立上幾分鐘，便能聽見由這些水流演奏出的超凡的交響樂，彷彿一隊沒有燈光的交響樂隊，在沼地的遠近各處，一齊奏起了形形色色的音響。在一處腐爛的低壩的洞穴裏，水流發出朗朗的吟誦聲；在小溪的一條支流沖過一道石擋土牆，向下傾瀉的地方，水流發出歡快的顫音；在拱橋下方，水流奏出金屬的鐃鈸聲；而在德爾諾弗洞裏，水流在嘁嘁地響着。水流聲最為響亮的，是一處叫十閘門的地方。到了仲春時節，這個地方發出的音響簡直就是一首賦格曲了。

（英）哈代：《卡斯特橋市長》

70   The Waters of the Danube

Nikolai Rostov turned aside and, as if searching for something, gazed into the distance, at the waters of the Danube, at the sky, and at the sun. How beautiful the sky looked, how blue, how calm, how deep! How brilliant and triumphant the setting sun! How sweetly shimmering the waters of the distant Danube! And fairer still the faraway blue mountains beyond the river, the nunnery, the mysterious ravines, the pine forests veiled to the treetops in mist ... there all was peaceful, happy.... "I could wish for nothing, nothing, if only I were there," thought Rostov.

Lev Tolstoy: War and Peace

七十　多瑙河之波

　　尼古拉‧羅斯托夫轉過身來。好像在尋找着甚麼，他凝
視着遠方，望着多瑙河的波浪，望着天空和太陽。天空看
去多麼美麗，多麼蔚藍，多麼寧靜，多麼深沉！夕陽是多
麼壯麗和輝煌啊！遙遠的多瑙河裏的水波閃爍得多麼溫柔
啊！更加美麗的是多瑙河邊遠處藍色的山巒、修道院、神
秘的深谷、樹頂煙霧繚繞的松樹林……那裏，一切都是那
麼寧靜和幸福……"我要是能在那裏，便再沒有甚麼希冀
了"羅斯托夫心想。

（俄）列夫‧托爾斯泰：《戰爭與和平》

71 The Beautiful Rhineland

Pleasant Rhine gardens! Fair scenes of peace and
sunshine — noble purple mountains, whose crests are
reflected in the magnificent stream — who has ever seen
you that has not a grateful memory of those scenes of friendly
repose and beauty?[1] To lay down the pen and even to think
of that beautiful Rhineland makes one happy. At this time of
summer evening, the cows are trooping down from the hills,
lowing and with their bells tinkling, to the old town, with its
old moats, and gates, and spires, and chestnut-trees, with long
blue shadows stretching over the grass; the sky and the river
below flame in crimson and gold; and the moon is already
out, looking pale towards the sunset. The sun sinks behind
the great castle-crested mountains, the night falls suddenly,
the river grows darker and darker, lights quiver in it from the
windows in the old ramparts, and twinkle peacefully in the
villages under the hills on the opposite shore.

W.M. Thackeray: Vanity Fair

1.　who...that... ：這是一種特殊句型，表達〝凡是……，誰不……〞的
　　意思。有時也可見到這樣的表達法：Who that has ever heard her
　　sing does not admire her？聽過她唱歌的人，有誰不羨慕？

七十一　萊茵河美景

　　萊茵河上的花園多麼可愛！周圍的景色是一片安寧，一片陽光──紫色的山巒氣勢雄偉，峯頂倒映在壯麗的河面上──凡是見過你的人，誰不留戀那番景色的親切、恬靜和美麗？擱下筆來，想想萊茵河一帶的美景，心裏頓覺愉快。夏季傍晚的這個時分，成羣結隊的母牛從山上下來，哞哞地叫着，脖子上的小鈴兒叮叮噹噹地響，都回到這古城裏來。那裏有年代久遠的護城河，古色古香的城門、尖塔和栗樹。每到日落時分，草地上印出長長的藍色影子，天上和底下的河面都泛起一片金紅色；月亮已經出來了，相對於落日，顯得素淡。太陽從山頂上的古堡後面沉落下去，黑夜驟然降臨，河水變得越來越幽暗。從年深日久的壁壘的窗口透出的燈光，投在河面上閃閃抖動，河對岸山腳下的村莊裏，也有燈光在靜靜地閃爍着。

　　　　　　　　　　　　（英）薩克雷：《名利場》

72   The Cherry-red Afterglow

In the evenings the cherry-red afterglow burned in the west. The moon rose from behind a lofty poplar. Its light spread over the Don in a cold white flame, broken into reflections and pools of black where the wind rippled the water. At night, blended with the murmur of the water, the cries of innumerable flocks of northward-flying geese sounded incessantly over the island. The birds, with no one to disturb them, often settled on the eastern side of the island. Over the backwaters, through the inundated forest the male teal called challengingly, ducks quacked, the barnacles and geese quietly cackled and answered one another. One day, noiselessly making his way to the bank, Grigory saw a large flock of swans not far from the island. The sun had not yet risen. The morning glow was flickering brilliantly beyond the barrier[1] of the forest. Reflecting its light, the water seemed rosy, and the great, majestic birds, with their heads turned to the sunrise, seemed rose-coloured also. Hearing a rustle on the bank, they flew up with a sonorous trumpet-call, and when they rose above the forest, Grigory was dazzled by the astonishing gleam of their snowy plumage.

Mikhail A. Sholokhov: And Quiet Flows the Don

七十二　殷紅的晚霞

　　每到傍晚，西方天際就出現一片櫻桃紅的晚霞。月亮
從一棵高高的白楊樹後面升了起來，月光像一股寒冷蒼白
的火燄在頓河上方照耀着。每當微風吹過，有漣漪的水面
就閃爍出月亮的反光和深潭似的黑影。夜晚，往北飛行的
無數雁羣在小島上空不停地叫着，跟河水的淙淙聲交織成
一片。這些無人驚擾的鳥兒們常常停落在小島的東邊。在
一些靜水處，在被水淹沒的林子裏，許多野公鴨發出求偶
的叫喚聲，母鴨子們呱呱地叫着。北極鵝和大雁在輕輕地
咕咕叫，互相應和着。一天，葛利高里悄然來到岸邊，在
離島不遠處看到了一大羣天鵝。太陽還未升起，林子遠處
的河面上泛出耀眼的晨曦，河水掩映着霞光，變成了玫瑰
色。許多威風凜凜的大鳥，腦袋都朝着日出的方向，彷彿
也染成了玫瑰色。大鳥一聽見岸上沙沙的腳步聲，便發出
銅號似的宏亮叫聲，紛紛飛離了河面。牠們飛越過樹林的
時候，葛利高里看見那雪白的羽毛十分耀眼。

　　　　　　　　　　　　（俄）肖洛霍夫：《靜靜的頓河》

---

1. barrier：原意“障礙”，這裏指擋住陽光的東西。

73 The Twilight Dream

In the dying day he would lean against the parapet of the embankment and look down at the rushing river, the fused and fusing[1], heavy, opaque, and hurrying mass, which was always like a dream of the past, wherein nothing could be clearly seen but great moving veils, thousands of streams, currents, eddies twisting into form, then fading away: it was like the blurred procession[2] of mental images in a fevered mind: forever taking shape, forever melting away. Over this twilight dream there skimmed phantom ferryboats, like coffins, with never a human form in them. Darker grew the night. The river became bronze. The lights upon its banks made its armor[3] shine with an inky blackness, casting dim reflections, the coppery reflections of the gas lamps, the moon-like reflections of the electric lights, the blood-red reflections of the candles in the windows of the houses. The river's murmur filled the darkness with its eternal muttering that was far more sad than the monotony of the sea....

Romain Rolland: Jean Christophe

---

1. fused and fusing：指河水交融匯合，喻腦海裏混雜的形象。

七十三　黄昏夢境

　　黄昏日落的時候，他常在堤岸上憑欄眺望，看着下面
洶湧奔騰的河水匯聚交融，混沌一片，望去沉重而幽暗，
老是奔流不息，總像是昔日的一個夢幻，從中甚麼也看不
清，只見片片巨大的移動的絹紗，成千上萬條小溪、激
流、漩渦，不停地生成，又不停地消失；那情景很像迷亂
的腦袋裏不斷湧起的一連串模糊的形象，永遠在那裏產
生，又永遠化為烏有。在這個黄昏的夢境中，像靈柩一樣
飄流着一些幻影似的渡船，上面見不到一個人影。暮色漸
濃，河流變成了大塊青銅，在兩岸燈光照耀下漆黑如墨的
河水閃出暗光，掩映着煤氣燈黄銅色的光，電燈蒼白色的
光，住家窗子裏血紅色的燭光。河水低低的喁語給黑夜增
添了無休無止的嗟怨，比沉悶單調的大海來得更淒涼……

　　　　（法）羅曼·羅蘭：《約翰·克利斯朵夫》

2.　procession：原義 "行列"。這裏指前仆後繼，不斷湧起的（模糊的
　　形象）。

3.　armor：原義 "盔甲"，這裏喻指河水的烏亮。

74　The Iridescent Surface of the Lake

The quiet, glassy, iridescent surface of this lake that now to both seemed, not so much like water as oil — like molten glass that, of enormous bulk and weight, resting upon the substantial earth so very far below. And the lightness and freshness and intoxication of the gentle air blowing here and there, yet scarcely rippling the surface of the lake. And the softness and furry thickness[1] of the tall pines about the shore. Everywhere pines — tall and spearlike. And above them the humped[2] backs of the dark and distant Adirondacks[3] beyond. Not a rower to be seen. Not a house or cabin. He sought to distinguish the camp of which the guide had spoken. He could not. He sought to distinguish the voices of those who might be there — or any voices. Yet, except for the lock-lock[4] of his own oars as he rowed and the voice of the boathouse keeper and the guide in converse two hundred, three hundred, five hundred, a thousand feet behind, there was no sound.

Theodore Dreiser: <u>An American Tragedy</u>

1.　furry thickness：像厚厚的毛。
2.　humped：隆起的，像駝峯的。

七十四　幻彩湖面

　　他們兩人這時看來，那平靜的，玻璃似的，彩虹色的湖面，與其說是像水，不如說是像油，像一大灘熔化了的玻璃，重重地壓在深深厚厚，結結實實的地球上。這裏那裏，不時颳起陣陣清新、柔和的微風，多麼令人陶醉。可是，湖面上並沒有吹起漣漪；湖岸上高高的松樹多麼柔和，多麼濃密。這裏，隨處都可見到高聳挺拔，像尖尖的劍戟一樣的松林。松林頂上，看得見遠處黛色的阿迪朗戴克斯山脈的駝峯。湖上見不到一個划船的人，岸上連一所房子，一間小木屋也看不到。他嘗試尋找那個嚮導提到的那個營幕，可是看不見。他嘗試尋找可能有人在那裏的說話聲，或者別的甚麼聲音，可是，除了他自己划船時雙槳發出的嘩啦嘩啦聲，和後面二百呎外、三百呎外、五百呎外、一千呎外看船屋的人和嚮導談話的聲音之外，甚麼聲音也沒有。

（美）德萊塞：《美國的悲劇》

3.　Adirondacks：阿迪朗戴斯山，美國紐約州東北部的山脈，介於聖勞倫斯河、尚普倫湖、安大略湖與摩霍克谷地之間。

4.　lock-lock：這裏作擬聲詞，模仿在湖中划船時雙槳發出的聲音。

75   The Bright White Sails

And then this scene, where a bright sun poured a flood of crystal light upon a greensward[1] that stretched from tall pines to the silver rippling waters of a lake. And off shore in a half dozen different directions the bright white sails of small boats — the white and green and yellow splashes of color[2], where canoes paddled by idling lovers were passing in the sun! Summertime — leisure — warmth — color — ease — beauty — love — all that he had dreamed of the summer before, when he was so very much alone.

Theodore Dreiser: <u>An American Tragedy</u>

---

1. greensward：草地，草皮
2. the white and green and yellow splashes of color：濺潑起來的水花，透過白色、綠色和黃色的船體彷彿也染上了各種色彩。

七十五　湖上帆影

接着便有這麼一幕，明亮的太陽在一塊青草地上灑下一片水晶般璀璨的光輝，這片草地從高高的松林那邊一直延伸到泛着閃閃銀光的漣漪的湖水邊。湖面上，有六、七處不同地點但見小船上明亮的白帆——悠閒自在的情侶們在陽光下划着獨木舟，白色、綠色和黃色的船身濺起陣陣彩色的水花。夏季——逍遙——溫情——繽紛色彩——舒適——美人——愛情，這一切正是他在去年夏季非常寂寞的時刻所夢想的啊。

（美）德萊塞：《美國的悲劇》

76 The Dismal Marshes

It was a dark night, though the full moon rose as I left the enclosed lands, and passed out upon the marshes. Beyond their dark line there was a ribbon of clear sky, hardly broad enough to hold the red large moon. In a few minutes she had ascended out of that clear field, in among the piled mountains of cloud.

There was a melancholy wind, and the marshes were very dismal. A stranger would have found them insupportable, and even to me they were so oppressive that I hesitated, half-inclined to go back. But I knew them, and could have found my way on a far darker night, and had no excuse for returning, being there. So, having come there against my inclination, I went on against it.

Charles Dickens: Great Expectations

七十六　淒涼的沼地

　　我走出了圍堤，來到沼地的時候，雖然一輪明月已經升起，天色依然是黑洞洞的。沼地一望無際，到天邊形成了一條黑綫，黑綫處是一條清澈的藍天，窄得像一條絲帶，幾乎容不下那一輪又大又紅的月亮。月兒向上爬呀爬呀，沒幾分鐘功夫就越過了那道明淨的夜空，淹沒在雲山雲海之中。

　　夜風幽怨，沼地上十分淒涼，別說陌生人到此會覺得受不住，即使是我，也覺得壓抑難當。竟然猶豫起來，有點想掉轉頭往回走了。可是，我熟悉這片沼地，那怕夜色再黑些，也萬萬迷不了路。到了這兒，就沒有理由再往回走，既然是違着自己的性子來了，索性就違着自己的性子走下去。

(英) 狄更斯：《遠大前程》

77 The Beach

The tide was about halfway out. The beach was smooth and firm, and the sand yellow. I went into a bathing-cabin, undressed, put on my suit, and walked across the smooth sand to the sea. The sand was warm under bare feet. There were quite a few people in the water and on the beach. Out beyond where the headlands of the Concha almost met to form the harbor there was a white line of breakers and the open sea. Although the tide was going out, there were a few slow rollers. They came in like undulations[1] in the water, gathered weight of water, and then broke smoothly on the warm sand. I waded out. The water was cold. As a roller came I dove, swam out under water, and came to the surface with all the chill gone. I swam out to the raft, pulled myself up, and lay on the hot planks. A boy and girl were at the other end. The girl had undone the top strap of her bathing-suit and was browning her back. The boy lay face downward on the raft and talked to her. She laughed at things he said, and turned her brown back in the sun.

Ernest Hemingway: The Sun Also Rises

---

1. undulations：原義 "波動、起伏"，這裏喻指成波浪形前進的細浪。

七十七 海灘

潮水差不多退了一半，海灘平滑而堅實，沙粒黃澄澄的。我走進一間浴場更衣室，脫掉了衣服，穿上泳衣，走過平坦的沙灘，來到海邊。光腳踩在沙上感到暖烘烘的，海水裏和海灘上人都不少。康查灣兩端的海岬，幾乎相連，形成了一個港灣，海岬外是一道道白色的浪頭和開闊的大海。雖然恰逢退潮，仍然有一些緩緩而來的巨浪。它們來時如同海面上的滾滾細浪，逐漸地勢頭越來越大，掀起浪頭，最終在溫暖的沙灘上平滑地沖刷開來。我蹚水出海，海水很涼。當一個浪頭打過來時，我便潛入水中，從水底泅出浮上海面時，寒氣全消了。我向木排游去，撐起身子爬上浮台，躺在滾燙的木板上。木板的另一頭有一對少年男女，姑娘解開了游泳衣的背帶扣，在曬背。小夥子臉朝下躺在浮台上和她説話。他説的事逗得她發笑，沖着太陽轉過她那曬黑了的脊背。

(美)海明威：《太陽照常升起》

78　The Coast Melted into the Morning

A flush came into the sky, the wan moon, half-way down the west, sank into insignificance. On the shadowy land things began to take life, plants with great leaves became distinct. They came through a pass in the big, cold sandhills on to the beach. The long waste of foreshore[1] lay moaning under the dawn and the sea; the ocean was a flat dark strip with a white edge. Over the gloomy sea the sky grew red. Quickly the fire[2] spread among the clouds and scattered them. Crimson burned to orange, orange to dull gold, and in a golden glitter the sun came up, dribbling fierily over the waves in little splashes, as if someone had gone along and the light had spilled from her pail as she walked.

The breakers ran down the shore in long, hoarse strokes. Tiny seagulls, like specks of spray, wheeled above the line of surf. Their crying seemed larger than they. Far away the coast reached out, and melted into the morning, and the tussocky[3] sandhills seemed to sink to a level with the beach.

1.　foreshore：漲潮則淹，退潮則顯的海灘；高潮綫和低潮綫中間的海岸。

2.　fire：喻指前面提及的紅彤彤的天空。

230

七十八　沙灘黎明

　　天空泛出一片紅光，蒼白的月亮已經沉入西邊一半的
天際，不久便消失了。幽暗的大地上各種有生命的物體開
始活躍起來，大葉子的植物變得清晰可辨。它們是穿越過
巨大而寒冷的沙丘上的一處豁口來到沙灘上的。那段長長
的漲灘空曠荒涼，在黎明的海水中嗚咽；此時的大海是一
條平平的，鑲着白邊的深色帶子。在陰沉沉的海面上，天
空逐漸露出了紅色。這片火很快在雲塊間蔓延，終於把雲
團驅散開去。緋紅的天空燒成了橙紅，又從橙紅變成了淡
金黃色，太陽便在這片燦爛金光中躍了出來。它將火紅的
光芒一小把一小把地滴灑到波濤的浪尖上，像是有人提着
桶走過，這光芒一路上從她的桶裏溢灑出來一般。

　　碎浪一下一下沖刷着長長的海灘，發出低沉沙啞的聲
響。形似點點浪花的小海鷗，迎着排浪在空中翻飛，它們
發出的叫聲似乎要比它們的身體大得多。遠處的海岸一直
向前方伸展開去，和清晨融為一體。長滿草叢的沙丘彷彿
變矮了，和沙灘似乎處於同一水平綫上。在沙丘右邊的梅

3.　tussocky：覆有草叢的，多草叢的。

Mablethorpe was tiny on their right. They had alone the space of all this level shore, the sea, and the upcoming sun, the faint noise of the waters, the sharp crying of the gulls.

...

The morning was of a lovely limpid gold colour. Veils of shadow[4] seemed to be drifting away on the north and the south. Clara stood shrinking slightly from the touch of the wind, twisting her hair. The sea-grass rose behind the white stripped woman.

...

She went plodding heavily over the sand that was soft as velvet. He, on the sandhills, watched the great pale coast envelop her. She grew smaller, lost proportion, seemed only like a large white bird toiling forward.

"Not much more than a big white pebble on the beach, not much more than a clot of foam being blown and rolled over the sand," he said to himself.

She seemed to move very slowly across the vast sounding shore. As he watched, he lost her. She was dazzled out of sight by the sunshine. Again he saw her, the merest white speck moving against the white, muttering sea-edge.

---

4. veils of shadow：像重重面紗般的黑影；這裏比喻朦朧的霧。

布爾索普鎮顯得非常渺小。這一切全屬於他們：平坦的海
岸，大海，初升的朝陽，依稀可辨的海浪聲，海鷗的尖叫
聲。

　　……

　　清晨泛出美麗淡雅的金黃色，朦朧的霧靄從南、北兩
面緩緩地飄移開去。克拉拉盤着頭髮站在那裏，身軀在海
風的吹拂下微微地顫抖着，海草在這個赤裸着身子，皮膚
白晰的女人的身後浮現了出來。

　　……

　　她拖着沉甸甸的腳步，在像絲絨般柔軟的沙子上艱難
地前行。他站在沙丘上，看着她慢慢地淹沒在茫茫的沙灘
上。她變得越來越小，小得失去了比例，彷彿只像一隻大
白鳥，在吃力地向前移動。

　　“她不過是沙灘上的一塊白色的小圓石子，不過是一
堆被風吹上沙灘的泡沫，”他對自己說。

　　她像是在非常緩慢地穿越那片寬廣而發出洪亮聲響的
海岸，他看着看着，便失去了她，眩目的陽光淹沒了她。
現在他又看到她了，僅僅是個小白點，在白色的，發出低
沉轟鳴聲的海邊緩緩移動。

"Look how little she is!" he said to himself. "She's lost like a grain of sand in the beach — just a concentrated speck blown along, a tiny white foam-bubble[5], almost nothing among the morning. Why does she absorb me?"

The morning was altogether uninterrupted: she was gone in the water. Far and wide the beach, the sandhills with their blue marram, the shining water, glowed together in immense, unbroken solitude.

D.H. Lawrence: <u>Sons and Lovers</u>

---

5. white foam-bubble：這裏的〝白色泡沫〞，連同前面出現過的〝沙子〞、〝大白鳥〞、〝小圓石子〞、〝濃縮點〞等等，都是鮮明、生動的意象，構成一幅優美生動的畫面。整段描寫情景交融，給人美不勝收的感受。

"看，她多麼渺小！"他對自己說，"她像粒遺忘在沙灘上的沙子——僅僅是被風颳着走的一個濃縮點，一個微小的白色泡沫。在這大清晨，彷彿甚麼都不是，她為甚麼會如此吸引我？"

　　早晨在延續，沒有受到任何干擾。她到大海中去了，一切都在永恆無垠的寂寥中閃閃發光——遼闊的沙灘，長着荒草的沙丘，還有波光粼粼的海水。

　　　　　　　　　（英）勞倫斯：《兒子和情人》

79 The Firmaments of Air and Sea

It was a clear steel-blue day. The firmaments[1] of air and sea were hardly separable in that all-pervading azure; only, the pensive air was transparently pure and soft, with a woman's look, and the robust and man-like sea heaved with long, strong, lingering swells, as Samson's[2] chest in his sleep.

Hither, and thither, on high, glided the snow-white wings of small, unspeckled birds; these were the gentle thoughts of the feminine air; but to and fro in the deeps, far down in the bottomless blue, rushed mighty leviathans[3], sword-fish, and sharks; and these were the strong, troubled, murderous thinkings of the masculine sea.

But though thus contrasting within, the contrast was only in shades and shadows without; those two seemed one; it was only the sex, as it were, that distinguished them.

---

1. firmaments：（文學用語）蒼穹，天空，通常作單數，並與定冠詞 the 連用。此處巧妙地比喻 air 和 sea 兩重天，故用複數。
2. Samson：參孫，聖經中人物，力大無比的勇士。
3. leviathans：聖經中的巨大海獸，如爬蟲或鯨。

七十九　海天交融

　　天空晴朗，呈鋼青色。在一片蔚藍中海天交融。只是默默沉思的天空既明淨又柔和，像個女人的臉；而那壯健、男人似的海洋，不停地起伏着，深沉、有力、遲緩，像是熟睡的參孫的胸脯。

　　在高空，這裏那裏，一些沒有斑點的小鳥展開雪白的翅膀在滑翔。這就是女性氣質的天空，令人遐思翩翩；可是，在海裏，在海的無底深淵中，游弋着巨大的鯨、劍魚和鯊魚；這些是男性氣質的大海，它激起人們強烈的、惱人的、殺氣騰騰的思想。

　　不過，雖然有如此內在的鮮明對照，外表的不同卻只是朦朦朧朧，影影綽綽的，這兩種東西彷彿只是一個：區分它們的似乎只是性別而已。

Aloft, like a royal czar and king, the sun seemed giving this gentle air[4] to this bold and rolling sea; even as bride to groom. And at the girdling line of the horizon — denoted the fond, throbbing trust, the loving alarms, with which the poor bride gave her bosom away.

Herman Melville: <u>Moby Dick</u>

---

4. air：這裏的 "air" 有相關語的作用，既指色彩、氣氛，也回應了前述的天空 (air)。句末更以新娘和新郎比喻海天的融合。

高高在上的太陽，像個威風凜凜的帝王，彷彿給這個豪邁翻騰的大海抹上了一層柔和的色彩；尤如新娘給予新郎的柔媚。而在腰帶似的地平綫上，有一陣多情的顫動——那個可憐的新娘在獻出她的身心時那種迷戀、鍾情的激動。

　　　　　　　　　　（美）麥爾維爾：《白鯨》

80 A Silvery Jet

Days, weeks passed, and under easy sail, the ivory
Pequod had slowly swept across four several cruising-
grounds[1]; that off[2] the Azores[3]; cff the Cape de Verdes[4], on
the Plate[5] (so called), being off the mouth of the Rio de la
Plata; and the Carrol Ground, an unstaked, watery locality,
southerly from St. Helena.

It was while gliding through these latter waters that one
serene and moonlight night, when all the waves rolled by
like scrolls of silver; and, by their soft, suffusing seethings[6],
made what seemed a silvery silence, not a solitude: on such
a silent night a silvery jet was seen far in advance of the
white bubbles at the bow. Lit up by the moon, it looked
celestial; seemed some plumed and glittering god uprising
from the sea.

Herman Melville: Moby Dick

---

1. cruising-grounds：原義為 "游弋地帶"，這裏指 fishing grounds，
   漁場。
2. that off...：這裏的 that 意義上 = that is；off 和 on 都表示船在……
   海面上。
3. Azores：亞速爾，北大西洋的羣島，屬葡萄牙。
4. Cape de Verdes：佛得角，非洲極西部一個角。

八十　銀白色的噴水

　　象牙色的"裴廓德號"一帆風順，經過了許多天，許多個星期的航行，慢慢地駛過了四個不同的漁場：那就是：亞速爾海面；佛得角海面；那個因為是在拉普拉塔河口而稱為普拉特；和那在聖海倫那南邊未立界的水域的卡羅爾漁場。

　　就在駛過這些水域的時候，在一個靜謐的月夜，波濤滾滾似銀軸，海浪在徐徐翻動，周圍彌漫一種不是孤寂，而是銀白色的靜穆；就在這樣靜穆的夜空裏，在浪花四濺的船頭的遠前方，出現了一股銀白色的噴水。在月光照耀下，賽似一道靈光，彷彿一個佩戴着翎飾，光耀奪目的神明從海裏冒上來。

(美) 麥爾維爾：《白鯨》

5.　Plate：普拉特河，在烏拉圭和阿根廷間的河口。" being off..."短句表示何以稱其為普拉特河的原因。整段是由二個由 and 連接的並列子句構成的長句。

6.　soft, suffusing seethings：suffusing 原義"充滿"，seethings 指"沸騰"，這裏比喻大片徐徐翻動的浪濤。值得留意的是"s"字／音的重疊運用，是英語中頭韻法的修辭手段 (alliteration)。此句前後尚有同樣的例子，如 scrolls of silver，silvery silence，solitude。

81　A Bonnie Island

They both halted on the green brow of the Common: they looked down on the deep valley robed in May raiment[1]; on varied meads[2], some pearled with daisies, and some golden with king-cups: to-day all this young verdure smiled clear in sunlight; transparent emerald and amber gleams played over it. On Nunnwood — the sole remnant of antique British forest in a region whose lowlands were once all sylvan chase, as its highlands were breast-deep heather — slept the shadow of a cloud; the distant hills were dappled, the horizon was shaded and tinted like mother-of-pearl; silvery blues, soft purples, evanescent greens and rose-shades, all melting into fleeces of white cloud, pure as azury snow, allured the eye as with a remote glimpse of heaven's foundations. The air blowing on the brow was fresh, and sweet, and bracing.

"Our England is a bonnie island," said Shirley, "and Yorkshire is one of her bonniest nooks."

Charlotte Brontë: Shirley

1.　raiment：（古語和詩歌用語）衣服、服飾總稱。
2.　meads：（詩歌用語）草地。

八十一　美麗的島國

　　他們兩人在公地蒼翠的陡坡上停了下來，俯視着下邊穿着五月盛裝的山谷。在各式各樣的草地上，有的長滿了雛菊，彷彿鑲了珍珠；有的滿地鱗莖毛茛，一片金黃。今天，所有這些青翠欲滴的草木都在陽光裏笑逐顏開；透明的翡翠色和琥珀般的光綫在它們上面嬉戲。一抹雲霞棲息在南林上——這是英國古代森林的唯一遺迹，這一地區的低地曾經都是林木茂盛的狩獵場，高地則都長滿高及胸膛的石楠。遠處山崗斑斑駁駁，地平綫影影綽綽，染上了珍珠母似的顏色，有銀藍色的、淡紫色的、淡綠色和玫瑰色的，這一切都化為朵朵白雲，純淨得如晴空白雪，彷彿要讓人一睹遙遠的天宮的台階那樣誘人眼目。山崗上風兒清爽怡人。

　　"我們英格蘭是個美麗的島國，"謝利説，"約克夏又是她最美麗的一個隱蔽去處。"

　　　　　　　　　　（英）夏洛蒂・勃朗特：《謝利》

82 Very Peaceful Land

Silvery fat barrage balloons[1], shining in the cloudless sky ahead of the plane before land came in view, gave the approach[2] to the British Isles a carnival touch. The land looked very peaceful in the fine August weather. Automobiles and lorries crawled on narrow roads, through rolling yellow-and-green patchwork fields marked off by dark hedgerows. Tiny sheep were grazing; farmers like little animated dolls were reaping corn. The plane passed over towns and cities clustered around gray spired cathedrals, and again over streams, woods, moors, and intensely green hedge-bounded fields, the pleasant England of the picture books, the paintings, and the poems.

Herman Wouk: The Winds of War

---

1. barrage balloons：阻禦敵機空襲用的阻塞汽球。
2. approach：通道，入門途徑；這裏譯作 "大門"。

八十二 平靜的原野

　　陸地未進視野之前，只見飛機前方萬里無雲的晴空中飄着銀光閃閃，脹鼓鼓的阻塞汽球，給英倫三島的大門平添了節日的氣氛。在八月的晴朗天氣裏，原野顯得分外平靜。汽車、貨車在窄窄的路面上緩緩爬行，穿越過波浪起伏的田野，這些田野被深暗的灌木籬笆分成青一塊、黃一塊，像是拼綴而成的。小小的羊羣在吃草，農民們像一些活動的小木偶那樣在收割玉米。飛機飛過羣集在各個灰色尖頂大教堂周圍的大城小鎮，飛過河流、樹林、沼地和一塊塊圍着籬笆的綠油油的田野，飛過那畫冊中、油畫上和詩歌裏描寫的可愛的英格蘭。

　　　　　　　　　　　（美）赫爾曼・沃克：《戰爭風雲》

Other Scenery
其他景物

83 National Aroma

A period of bad weather had settled down upon Gardencourt; the days grew shorter, and there was an end to the pretty tea-parties on the lawn. But Isabel had long indoor conversations with her fellow-visitor, and in spite of the rain the two ladies often sallied forth for a walk, equipped with the defensive apparatus which the English climate and the English genius have between them brought to such perfection. Madame Merle was very appreciative[1]; she liked almost everything, including the English rain. "There is always a little of it, and never too much at once," she said; "and it never wets you, and it always smells good." She declared that in England the pleasures of smell were great — that in this inimitable[2] island there was a certain mixture of fog and beer and soot which, however odd it might sound, was the

---

1. appreciative：有欣賞力的。這一詞在這裏的用法是值得玩味的，具有明顯的諷刺口吻。常人認為進入雨季是英國的"bad weather"，可是，梅爾夫人於壞天氣中也能欣賞到某種妙處，充分顯示了她的"高超"之處。作家詹姆斯一生傾心於"國際題材"(international theme) 的研究，時時處處將世界跟歐洲大陸作對比，常有精闢獨到的評論。《一位女士的畫像》是體現這一研究的代表作，上述所選的段落是一生動的例子。

八十三　國香

　　花園山莊進入了陰雨綿綿的時期，白晝日漸見短，草坪上令人愉快的茶會已經停止。但是，伊莎貝爾常在室內跟她的同伴長談，有時兩位女士也不顧下雨，帶上防雨用具外出散步——英國的氣候和英國的天才可說已經將這種用具發展到盡善盡美的地步。梅爾夫人是頗具賞識力的；她幾乎甚麼都喜歡，包括英國的雨天在內。"這裏常常下點小雨，又從來不一下子下得太多，"她說，"它從不把你淋濕，而且總是夾帶一股清新的氣息。"她宣稱，在英國常可獲得一種嗅覺上極大的快感——在這個舉世無雙的島國，到處飄浮着霧、啤酒和煤煙混合而成的氣味，不論

---

2. inimitable：無法仿效的。

national aroma, and was most agreeable to the nostril; and she used to lift the sleeve of her British overcoat and bury her nose in it, to inhale the clear, fine odour of the wool.

Henry James: *The Portrait of a Lady*

聽起來有多古怪，卻是一種國香，聞起來總是特別舒適。
她常常舉起穿着的那件英國大衣的衣袖，把鼻子湊上去，
聞聞那股清新、美好的羊毛衫味。

（美）亨利·詹姆斯：《一位女士的畫像》

84   The Chalet

That fall the snow came very late. We lived in a brown
wooden house in the pine trees on the side of the mountain
and at night there was frost so that there was thin ice over the
water in the two pitchers on the dresser in the morning. Mrs.
Guttingen came into the room early in the morning to shut
the windows and started a fire in the tall porcelain stove.
The pine wood crackled and sparked and then the fire roared
in the stove and the second time Mrs. Guttingen came into
the room she brought big chunks of wood for the fire and a
pitcher of hot water. When the room was warm she brought
in breakfast. Sitting up in bed eating breakfast we could see
the lake and the mountains across the lake on the French
side. There was snow on the tops of the mountains and the
lake was a gray steel-blue.

Outside, in front of the chalet[1] a road went up the
mountain. The wheel ruts and ridges were iron hard with the
frost, and the road climbed steadily through the forest and
up and around the mountain to where there were meadows,

---

1. chalet：瑞士農舍小屋。

八十四　瑞士湖光山色

　　那年秋天，雪姗姗來遲。我們住在山邊松林中的一所褐色的木房子裏。夜晚上霜，一到早晨，放在梳妝枱上的那兩瓶水便結着一層薄冰。房東葛天根太太一大早就進屋來，先關好窗子，接着就在那高高的瓷爐上升起了火。松木劈啪作響，閃着火花，不久便火光熊熊。房東太太第二次進屋來時，帶來一瓶熱水和添火用的大塊木頭。等屋子暖和後她送來了早飯。坐在牀上吃早飯時，我們可以望見湖水，和湖對岸法國那邊的山峯。山頂上積着雪，湖水是鋼青色中略呈灰色。

　　屋外，房子前面有一條上山的路，車轍和山嶺都被霜凍得硬梆梆的。路穿過樹林往上走，繞過山，一直通到樹

and barns and cabins in the meadows at the edge of the woods looking across the valley. The valley was deep and there was a stream at the bottom that flowed down into the lake and when the wind blew across the valley you could hear the stream in the rocks.

Sometimes we went off the road and on a path through the pine forest. The floor of the forest was soft to walk on; the frost did not harden it as it did the road. But we did not mind the hardness of the road because we had nails in the soles and heels of our boots and the heel nails bit on the frozen ruts and with nailed boots it was good walking on the road and invigorating. But it was lovely walking in the woods.

In front of the house where we lived the mountain went down steeply to the little plain along the lake and we sat on the porch of the house in the sun and saw the winding of the road down the mountain-side and the terraced vineyards on the side of the lower mountain, the vines all dead now for the winter and the fields divided by stone walls, and below the vineyards the houses of the town on the narrow plain along the lake shore. There was an island with two trees on

林邊有草地的地方。草地上有倉房和小房子，面對着山谷。山谷很深，谷底有一條小溪流入湖裏。每當山谷裏颳過一陣清風，便可以聽見石間的流水聲。

有時我們離開大路，踏上一條穿過松林的小徑。松林裏的地沒有凍得像路面那麼硬，踏上去較鬆軟。我們倒也不怕路面的堅硬，因為我們的靴子的前後掌上都釘了釘子、鞋釘扎進冰凍的路面，穿這樣的鞋走路，既舒適又省力。誠然，在林中散步是令人愉快的事。

我們所住的小屋前面，山勢陡峭，直插湖邊的一塊小平原。有時，我們坐在門廊裏曬太陽，眺望山腰上蜿蜒的山路，和那些矮山上層層梯形的葡萄園。籐蔓在冬天都早已枯死了，葡萄園中間都有石牆隔開。葡萄園下方，是沿着湖岸一條窄地而建的城裏的房子。湖上有個小島，島上

the lake and the trees looked like the double sails of a fishing-boat. The mountains were sharp and steep on the other side of the lake and down at the end of the lake was the plain of the Rhône[2] Valley flat between the two ranges of mountains; and up the valley where the mountains cut it off was the Dent du Midi. It was a high snowy mountain and it dominated the valley but it was so far away that it did not make a shadow.

Ernest Hemingway: <u>A Farewell to Arms</u>

---

2. Rhône：羅納河。法國第二大河，發源於瑞士南部阿爾卑斯山的聖哥大，在法、瑞邊境瀦為日內瓦湖。沿河兩岸工業城鎮林立，多種植葡萄。

有兩棵樹，遠遠望去像是漁船的雙帆。湖對岸的高山都很險峻陡峭，山腳下的湖邊盡頭處是羅納河谷，是夾在兩列山脈之間的一塊平地；山谷上端異峯突起，那是唐都米蒂，一座高高的，控制着整個山谷的雪山。不過，距離太遠，看不見投下的影子。

（美）海明威：《永別了，武器》

85　More Eden-like Nook

I walked a while on the pavement; but a subtle, well-known scent — that of a cigar — stole from some window; I saw the library casement open a hand-breadth; I knew I might be watched thence; so I went apart into the orchard. No nook in the grounds more sheltered and more Eden-like; a very high wall shut it out from the court on one side; on the other a beech avenue screened it from the lawn. At the bottom was a sunk fence, its sole separation from lonely fields: a winding walk, bordered with laurels and terminating in a giant horse-chestnut, circled at the base by a seat, led down to the fence. Here one could wander unseen. While such honeydew fell, such silence reigned, such gloaming gathered, I felt as if I could haunt such shade for ever; but in treading the flower and fruit parterres at the upper part of the enclosure, enticed there by the light the now rising moon cast on this more open quarter, my step is stayed — not by sound, not by sight, but once more by a warning fragrance.

Sweet-brier and southernwood, jasmine, pink, and rose have long been yielding their evening sacrifice[1] of incense:

---

1. sacrifice：原義 "奉獻"，"貢獻"；這裏喻指發出芳香。

八十五　賽似伊甸園

　　我在庭院小徑上散了一會兒步；可是一陣淡淡的、熟悉的氣味——雪茄煙味——從附近一扇窗戶中飄了出來。我瞧見圖書館的窗開着有一手寬的光景；我知道可能有人從那裏窺視，我便走開，到果園去。庭院裏再也沒有別的角落，比這裏更加隱蔽，更似伊甸園了。一面由一堵高牆把它和院子隔開，另一邊，一條掬樹林蔭道屏障，把它和草坪分開。盡頭是一道坍塌了的籬笆，這是庭院和孤寂的田野的唯一分界綫；一條蜿蜒小徑通向籬笆，沿路都是月桂樹。路的盡頭是一棵高大的歐洲七葉樹，繞着樹底有一圈坐位。在這兒，可以漫步而不被人看見。蜜露降臨，萬籟俱寂，暮色漸濃，我覺得彷彿可以永遠在這樣的樹蔭裏散步下去；可是，當我徜徉於園子較高處的花叢和果壇間，來到這處受初升的月亮照射的開闊地時，我不由自主地停住了腳步——不是被聲音，不是被景象，而是再一次被一種警告性的香味阻住了。

　　香薔薇、青蒿、茉莉、石竹、玫瑰，一直都是在夜間

this new scent is neither of shrub nor flower; it is — I know it well — it is Mr. Rochester's cigar. I look round and listen. I see trees laden with ripening fruit. I hear a nightingale warbling in a wood half a mile off: no moving form is visible, no coming step audible; but that perfume increases: I must flee. I make for the wicket leading to the shrubbery, and I see Mr. Rochester entering. I step aside into the ivy recess; he will not stay long: he will soon return whence he came, and if I sit still he will never see me.

But no — eventide is as pleasant to him as to me, and this antique garden as attractive; and he strolls on, now lifting the gooseberry-tree branches to look at the fruit, large as plums, with which they are laden; now taking a ripe cherry from the wall; now stooping towards a knot of flowers, either to inhale their fragrance or to admire the dew-beads on their petals. A great moth goes humming by me; it alights on a plant at Mr. Rochester's foot: he sees it, and bends to examine it.

Charlotte Brontë: Jane Eyre

吐露芬芳：但這股新的香味，既不是灌木香又不是花香；那是——我很熟悉它——那是羅切斯特先生的雪茄的香味。我環顧四周，靜靜聽，我看到果樹掛滿了成熟的果子。我聽見一隻夜鶯，在半哩之外的樹林裏宛轉歌唱：看不見甚麼走動的人影，聽不見甚麼走近的腳步聲。可是，那股香味越來越濃；我必須趕緊溜走，我朝通向灌木叢的小門走去，卻看到羅切斯特先生正走了進來。我往旁邊一閃，躲進了常青藤的隱蔽處。他不會呆久，會很快回到所來之處去，只要我坐着不動，他絕不會看見我。

可是不——薄暮對他來說跟對我一樣地可愛，這個古色古香的花園對他也一樣地迷人；他信步而來，一會兒拉起醋栗樹枝，看看上面長着大得似梅子的累累碩果；一會兒從牆頭上摘下一隻熟透了的櫻桃；一會兒又朝花叢彎下腰去，不是去聞聞花香，就是去觀賞花瓣上的露珠兒。一隻大飛蛾嗡嗡地飛過我的身邊；牠停落在羅切斯特先生腳邊的一棵植物上；他看見了牠，朝牠彎下腰去仔細察看起來。

（英）夏洛蒂·勃朗特：《簡·愛》

86   A Dazzling Polychrome

The outskirt of the garden in which Tess found herself
had been left uncultivated for some years, and was now damp
and rank with juicy grass which sent up mists of pollen at a
touch; and with tall blooming weeds emitting offensive smells
— weeds whose red and yellow and purple hues formed a
polychrome[1] as dazzling as that of cultivated flowers. She
went stealthily as a cat through this profusion of growth,
gathering cuckoo-spittle on her skirts, cracking snails that
were underfoot, staining her hands with thistle-milk and slug-
slime, and rubbing off upon her naked arms sticky blights
which, though snow-white on the apple-tree trunks, made
madder stains[2] on her skin; thus she drew quite near to Clare,
still unobserved of him.

Thomas Hardy: Tess of the d'Urbervilles

---

1. polychrome：原義 彩色的藝術品"，這裏喻指多種顏色的鮮花，彷
    彿構成了一副五彩斑爛的畫面。

2. made madder stains：（madder 茜草）染上了顏色，（桔紅、鮮
    紅等）如同茜草根莖新染的顏色一般。

八十六　色彩絢麗的畫面

　　苔絲現在站着的地方，原來是園子的外圍，已有幾年沒有耕作過了。現在這裏一片潮濕，上面長滿了多汁的牧草，碰一下就會飛起一陣霧一般的花粉。還有開着花兒的高高的雜草，散發出一種難聞的氣味——它們的紅顏色、黃顏色和紫顏色，構成了一幅色彩絢麗的畫面，賽似百花園。她在這片花草叢生的茂密地裏，像隻貓似地輕輕走了過去，裙腳邊黏上了吐泡蟲的泡沫，腳底下踩碎了蝸牛殼，兩隻手染上了薊花的乳汁和蛞蝓的黏液，兩隻露着的胳膊也蹭上了黏糊糊的樹霉。這種東西，在蘋果樹樹幹上是雪白的，但是，到了皮膚上，就變成像茜草染料的顏色。她就這樣走着，已經十分靠近克萊爾，卻仍未被他看見。

　　　　　　　　　　　　（英）哈代：《德伯家的苔絲》

87   The Water of the Garden

They walked back to Yonville along the river. Its level
sank in summer, widening its banks and revealing the bottoms
of the walls of the gardens, each of which had a few steps
leading down to the water. It ran silently, swift and cold-
looking; long thin grass swayed with the current, like
disheveled green hair growing in its limpid depths. Here and
there an insect with delicate legs was crawling or sitting on a
water-lily leaf or the tip of a reed. Sunbeams pierced the
little blue bubbles which kept forming and bursting on the
ripples; branchless old willows mirrored their gray bark in
the water; the meadows around them seemed empty. It was
dinnertime on the farms. As the young woman and her
companion walked along they heard nothing but the rhythm
of their footsteps on the dirt path, the words they were saying
to each other and the sound of her dress rustling all around
her.

The garden walls, with their copings of pieces of broken
bottles, were as warm as the glass of a greenhouse.
Wallflowers had taken root between the bricks, and the edge

八十七　花園小溪

　　他們沿着河岸走回永鎮。到了夏季，河水低落，河岸
寬了起來，花園的牆基也裸露出來，幾處牆基都有幾級台
階通到水邊。河水靜靜地淌着，望過去覺得又快又涼爽，
一些細長的水草順流飄動，像是一把亂蓬蓬的綠頭髮，生
長在清澈的水裏。這裏那裏，有時會有一隻細腳蟲在睡蓮
的葉面上爬來爬去，或者坐在蘆葦尖上。陽光像根根細
絲，穿透一隻隻藍色的小水泡，這些小水泡不斷地生成，
又在漣漪中不斷地破碎。脫去了樹枝的老柳樹的灰色樹皮
在水中映了出來，周圍的草地空空蕩蕩，彷彿一無所有。
現在是農場用飯的時刻，萬籟俱寂，少婦和她的同伴在那
裏走着，只聽見他們走在小徑上的腳步聲，相互的談話
聲，和她的裙袍的窸窣聲。
　　花園牆頂砌有碎玻璃，牆面如同溫室玻璃窗那樣溫
暖。黃色牆花從磚頭的縫隙間長出。包法利夫人從旁走過

of Madame Bovary's open parasol crumbled some of their blossoms into yellow dust as she passed; or an overhanging branch of honeysuckle or clematis would catch on the fringe and brush against the silk for a moment.

Gustave Flaubert: Madame Bovary

時，她撐開的傘，傘邊觸及牆頭，就碰碎了一些黃花；要不就是有甚麼垂掛在牆邊的忍冬花或者鐵綫蓮的藤蔓刮着她的傘邊的流蘇，有時又蹭着陽傘的緞面。

(法) 福樓拜：《包法利夫人》

88 Ivory Roses

He followed her across the nibbled pasture in the dusk. There was a coolness in the wood, a scent of leaves, of honeysuckle, and a twilight. The two walked in silence. Night came wonderfully there, among the throng of dark tree-trunks. He looked round, expectant.

She wanted to show him a certain wild-rose bush she had discovered. She knew it was wonderful. And yet, till he had seen it, she felt it had not come into her soul. Only he could make it her own, immortal. She was dissatisfied.

Dew was already on the paths. In the old oak-wood a mist was rising, and he hesitated, wondering whether one whiteness were a strand of fog or only campion-flowers pallid in a cloud.

By the time they came to the pine-trees Miriam was getting very eager and very tense. Her bush might be gone. She might not be able to find it; and she wanted it so much. Almost passionately she wanted to be with him when he stood before the flowers. They were going to have a communion together — something that thrilled her, something holy. He was walking beside her in silence. They were very near to each other. She trembled, and he listened, vaguely anxious.

八十八　白玫瑰

在暮色中，他跟着她走過一片被牲口啃吃過的牧草地。樹林裏傳來一股清涼氣息，空氣中氤氳着樹葉和忍冬的清香，周圍泛着薄暮的微光。兩人默默地走着，美妙的夜色降臨到這片昏暗、密集的樹幹中。他環顧四周，彷彿期待着甚麼。

她想讓他看一叢她早些時候發現的野玫瑰，她知道那花非常美。然而，在他沒有看見它之前，她覺得這花依然沒有進入自己的心靈，只有他才能使這叢花變成她自己的，永遠不會凋謝的花。她感到掃興。

露水濡濕了小徑，老橡樹林裏已經升起一層薄薄的霧靄。他猶豫着，不知那一綹白花花的東西究竟是一團霧，還只是一簇模糊的蒼白的石竹花。

待他們來到松樹林時，米利安心裏越來越焦急和緊張，她的花叢很可能不見了，她也許找不到了，但她是多麼渴望着找到它啊！她幾乎是懷着一股激情，盼望着能跟他一起站在花前，他們就會共同擁有心靈交融的刹那——這將令她激動不已，給她一種神聖的感受。他在她身邊默默地走着，他們彼此離得很近，她顫抖了，而他傾聽着，模模糊糊地感到有些憂慮。

Coming to the edge of the wood, they saw the sky in front, like mother-of-pearl, and the earth growing dark. Somewhere on the outermost branches of the pine-wood the honeysuckle was streaming scent.

"Where?" he asked.

"Down the middle path," she murmured, quivering.

When they turned the corner of the path she stood still. In the wide walk between the pines, gazing rather frightened, she could distinguish nothing for some moments; the greying light robbed things of their colour. Then she saw her bush.

"Ah!"she cried, hastening forward.

It was very still. The tree was tall and straggling. It had thrown its briers over a hawthorn-bush, and its long streamers[1] trailed thick, right down to the grass, splashing the darkness everywhere with great spilt stars[2], pure white. In bosses[3] of ivory and in large splashed stars the roses gleamed on the darkness of foliage and stems and grass. Paul and Miriam stood close together, silent, and watched. Point

---

1. streamer：野玫瑰帶刺的枝條。

2. stars：原義 "星星"，這裏喻指一朵朵白玫瑰，在蒼茫的夜色中宛如閃爍的星星。本段句末用了同一意象，把 put out（義：淹沒或熄滅光輝）與 roses 連用，把玫瑰喻作星星。此外 spilt 解 "倒瀉了"，而這裏則有 "水銀瀉地" 的意味，跟下句的 splashed stars 意象相同。

來到樹林的邊緣時，他們看到前方的天際一片珍珠母似的色彩，大地越來越晦暗了，從松樹林最外邊的枝椏處，不斷飄來忍冬撲鼻的芳香。

　　"在哪兒呀？"他問。

　　"在中間那條小道上，"她聲音發顫地喃喃道。

　　當他們拐過小路後，她一動不動地站住了，在松林間的開闊地上，憂心忡忡地搜尋着。一時甚麼也分辨不出來，因為灰蒙蒙的光綫使一切東西都脫了色。突然，她發現了她的花叢。

　　"啊！"她喊道，並急忙奔上前。

　　四周萬籟俱寂，這簇花高大繁茂，多刺的枝條灑落在一棵山楂樹上；那些長長的枝條茂密地垂落到草地上，向四周黑暗拋灑出大顆潔白的星星。白玫瑰猶如玲瓏浮凸的象牙浮彫和水銀瀉地般的星星，在昏暗的樹葉、枝幹和草地上閃閃發光。保羅和米利安兩人站在一起，靜靜地觀看

3.　bosses：突起物，in bosses of ivory 意為許許多多如同象牙浮彫般的白玫瑰。

after point the steady roses shone out to them, seeming to
kindle something in their souls. The dusk came like smoke
around, and still did not put out the roses.

D.H. Lawrence: <u>*Sons and Lovers*</u>

着，那玫瑰不慌不忙地一朵朵向他們展示風姿，彷彿要點燃他們心靈中某種東西。夜色像煙霧似地籠罩了一切，但依然無法淹沒玫瑰的光輝。

（英）勞倫斯：《兒子和情人》

89　The Little Orchards

And all the time the fruit swells and the flowers break out in long clusters on the vines. And in the growing year the warmth grows and the leaves turn dark green. The prunes lengthen like little green birds' eggs, and the limbs sag down against the crutches under the weight. And the hard little pears take shape, and the beginning of the fuzz comes out on the peaches. Grape-blossoms shed their tiny petals and the hard little beads[1] become green buttons[2], and the buttons grow heavy. The men who work in the fields, the owners of the little orchards, watch and calculate. The year is heavy with produce. And men are proud, for of their knowledge they can make the year heavy[3]. They have transformed the world with their knowledge. The short, lean wheat has been made big and productive. Little sour apples have grown large and sweet, and that old grape that grew among the trees and fed

---

1. beads：原義 "小珠子"，這裏喻指只有小珠子那般大小的剛長出的葡萄。

2. buttons：喻指長成稍大些的像鈕釦般大小的葡萄。

3. heavy：這裏意為 "滿載的"， "make the year heavy" 使這一年豐產。

八十九　果園

　　果實時時都在長大，葡萄籐上長出了一長串一長串的
花兒。在這生長的季節裏，天氣漸漸熱了起來，樹葉變成
了深綠色，梅子變長了，像綠色的小鳥蛋似的。枝條讓沉
甸甸的果實壓得彎彎的，墜在撐杆上。梨子成形了，又小
又硬；桃子上開始長出了絨毛。葡萄花上細小的花瓣脫落
了，那些硬硬的小珠子變成綠色的鈕釦，這些"鈕釦"又
逐漸長大變得重重的。在果園勞作的人們，亦即小果園的
主人們，眼巴巴地望着，盤算着，這一年的出產定會是豐
富的。他們感到自豪，因為他們的知識經驗會給他們這年
帶來好收成。他們用自己的知識改造了世界，把矮小低產
的小麥變成高大而豐產；又小又酸的蘋果變成又大又甜。
那些原先長在樹林裏的古老的葡萄樹，果實只能餵鳥吃。

the birds, its tiny fruit has mothered a thousand varieties, red and black, green and pale pink, purple and yellow; and each variety with its own flavour. The men who work in the experimental farms have made new fruits: nectarines and forty kinds of plums, walnuts with paper shells. And always they work, selecting, grafting, changing, driving themselves, driving the earth to produce.

John Steinbeck: <u>The Grapes of Wrath</u>

如今，這些已經成了母樹，它的小小的種子已經嫁接出無數新品種，有紅的、黑的、綠的和淡紅的；紫的和黃的，每一品種都有自己獨特的口味。在實驗農場工作的人們培育出了新品種水果：蜜桃和四十種梅子，還有薄殼核桃。他們不停地忙着選種、嫁接、換種，老摧着自己多幹苦幹、催着土地增產。

（美）斯坦倍克：《憤怒的葡萄》

90　An Old-fashioned Little Village

It was as old-fashioned as it was small, and it rested in the lap of an undulating upland adjoining the North Wessex[1] downs[2]. Old as it was, however, the well-shaft was probably the only relic of the local history that remained absolutely unchanged. Many of the thatched and dormered[3] dwelling-houses had been pulled down of late years, and many trees felled on the green. Above all, the original church, hump-backed, wood-turreted, and quaintly hipped, had been taken down, and either cracked up into heaps of road-metal[4] in the lane, or utilized as pig-sty walls, garden seats, guard-stones to fences, and rockeries in the flowerbeds of the neighbourhood. In place of it a tall new building of modern Gothic design, unfamiliar to English eyes, had been erected on a new piece of ground by a certain obliterator[5] of historic

---

1. Wessex：維撒克斯，是本書背景的總名字，本意為 "西撒克斯"，是第十世紀前英國未統一時的五國之一。維撒克斯分為六部分，其中一部分為北維撒克斯，這兒提到的這片高原叫伊爾斯利丘陵。

2. downs：丘陵，常用複數。

3. dormered： = dormer window 建築用語，屋頂斜坡上凸出之天窗，屋頂窗。

九十 古老的村莊

　　這個村莊年代久遠，人家稀少。它坐落在與北維撒克斯丘陵相連接的那塊起伏高原中間的一個山坳裏。它雖然那樣古老，但是，在本地歷史流傳下來，而絲毫不變的古物中，恐怕只有那眼井的井筒子。近幾年來，那些屋頂開着天窗的茅草房都給鏟平了，許多長在綠草地上的大樹也都給伐倒了；最重要的是，原有那個有駝背屋脊，木建尖閣，和古雅別致斜頂的教堂，現在也拆除了；拆下來的材料，不是碾成了鋪路用的碎石塊，堆在小路邊，就是用作鄰近一帶砌豬圈的牆、園子裏的石椅、籬笆兩旁的護路石、或者堆成花壇裏的假山了。取而代之的，是一幢建在新的地址上的高高建築物——一幢普通英國人看來陌生的現代哥特式建築，它是由一個一天之內往返倫敦的歷史遺

---

4. road-metal：英國特有用語，鋪路用的碎石料。

5. obliterator：英國鄉土志作家哈帕在《哈代鄉土志》裏説，這個教堂建於 1866 年，設計者為斯特鋭特 (G.E.Street,1824-1881)。這裏他被哈代諷之為"歷史遺迹毀滅者"。

records[6] who had run down from London and back in a day. The site whereon so long had stood the ancient temple to the Christian divinities was not even recorded on the green and level grass-plot that had immemorially been the churchyard, the obliterated graves being commemorated by eighteen-penny cast-iron[7] crosses warranted to last five years.

Thomas Hardy: <u>Jude the Obscure</u>

6. records：原義 "記錄"，"記載"，這裏和 historic 連用，喻指歷史遺迹，跟上文的 relic 恰好呼應。

7. cast-iron：生鐵，鑄鐵。

迹毀滅者建造的。原先供奉基督教聖賢的那座年代久遠的
古廟，雖然曾經矗立了那麼久，如今，在那片平坦的青草
地上已經了無痕迹。那塊地從古以來曾經是教堂的院子；
豎立了管用五年、值十八便士的生鐵十字架為紀念的墳
地，也已經從人們的記憶中消失。

（英）哈代：《無名的裴德》

91 The Church

The church is on the other side of the street, twenty yards further on, at the entrance to the public square. The little cemetery surrounding it is so full of graves that the old tombstones, lying flat on the ground, form a continuous pavement on which the grass has traced out green rectangles. The church was rebuilt during the latter part of the reign of Charles X. The arched wooden ceiling is beginning to rot at the top, and its blue surface is marred here and there by black cavities[1]. Above the door, where most churches have an organ, is a gallery for the men, reached by a spiral staircase which echoes beneath their wooden soles.

The daylight coming in through the plain glass windows falls obliquely on the pews[2] projecting from the wall. There are straw mats tacked on some of them with these words in big letters below: "Monsieur So-and-So's Pew." Further on, where the nave[3] narrows, is the confessional. Beside it stands

---

1. cavities：中空，洞。
2. pews：教堂裏的靠背長凳。
3. nave：早期教堂中殿（信眾座位所在部分）。

九十一　教堂

　　教堂在街的斜對面，再走二十碼的地方，把着公共廣場的入口處。四周圍繞教堂的公墓不大，裏面墓冢壘壘，舊的墓石平躺在地上，連接在一起，像是鋪地的石板，縫隙間已經長滿了荒草，一方一方的，綠茵成畦。查理十世在位後期，教堂曾經翻修一新，如今，弓形的木頂已經開始腐爛，表面塗着的藍顏色因木頭出現黑色中空而變得斑斑駁駁。大門上方，一般教堂安放風琴的地方，變成男人們聚會的門廊，有一螺旋形的樓梯盤旋而上，木頭鞋底踩上去，咯噔咯噔地響。

　　陽光透過單色的玻璃窗，斜照在教堂裏倚牆而擺的靠背長凳上。有些凳上釘上草墊，寫着如下幾個大字："某先生之凳"。再往裏去，教堂中殿狹窄處，有一懺悔間，

a statue of the Virgin; she is dressed in a satin gown and a tulle veil[4] sprinkled with silver stars, and her cheeks are painted bright red like an idol from the Sandwich Islands[5]. Finally, the view is terminated by a copied painting — "The Holy Family, Presented by the Minister of the Interior" — hanging above the main altar between four candlesticks.

Gustave Flaubert: Madame Bovary

---

4. tulle veil： （做面紗，婦女晚禮服用的）薄紗。
5. Sandwich Islands：Hawaiian Islands 的舊稱。

旁邊立着一尊聖母像。聖母身穿緞袍，頭上蒙着銀星點點的薄面紗，臉蛋漆成硃紅色，酷似夏威夷的一尊神像。最後，視野所及之處是一幅摹畫的油畫，上面寫着"神聖家庭——內政部部長贈"，掛在四隻燭台之間的聖壇的上方。

（法）福樓拜：《包法利夫人》

92 Garden Court

Her uncle's house seemed a picture made real; no refinement of the agreeable was lost[1] upon Isabel; the rich perfection of Gardencourt at once revealed a world[2] and gratified a need[3]. The large, low rooms, with brown ceilings and dusky corners, the deep embrasures[4] and curious casements[5], the quiet light on dark, polished panels, the deep greeness outside, that seemed always peeping in, the sense of well-ordered privacy, in the centre of a "property"— a place where sounds were felicitously accidental, where the tread was muffled by the earth itself, and in the thick mild air all shrillness dropped out of conversation — these things were much to the taste of our young lady, whose taste played a considerable part in her emotions.

Henry James: The Portrait of a Lady

---

1. no refinement of the agreeable was lost：這裏 refinement 解作 "精緻" 或 "精妙" 之處；agreeable 為 "令人愜意的" 或 "討人喜歡的" 事物。全句直譯為 沒有一樣令人愉快的美妙之處會逃過依莎貝爾的眼光"。
2. world：給人耳目一新的新天地。
3. need：這裏指人們心理上對美的需求和渴望。

九十二　花園山莊

　　姨父家的住屋，像是一幅變成為現實的圖畫，在依莎
貝爾的眼裏，樣樣都美不勝收，沒有不稱她的心的。多姿
多采的花園山莊別有洞天，讓人賞心悅目。那寬敞、低矮
的房間，那褐色的天花板和幽暗的角落，那深厚的，漏斗
形的邊牆和別致的門窗，那光滑的深色鑲板上發出的柔和
光綫，那屋外彷彿老是在往裏窺探的濃綠色調，那幢花園
住宅賦與的井然有序的隱秘感——在這個地方，難得聽到
一點聲音，腳步聲已被地面所吸收，在濃濃的溫煦之中，
一切刺耳的談話聲也都消失了——這些都非常吻合我們這
位少女的口味，而她的愛好對她的情感是舉足輕重的。

　　　　　　（美）亨利‧詹姆斯：《一位女士的畫像》

4.　embrasures：建築上指內寬外窄的門窗的邊牆。
5.　casement：兩扇對開的門式窗。

93   The Shadow

All that prospect, which from the terrace looked so near, has moved solemnly away, and changed — not the first nor the last of beautiful things[1] that look so near and will so change — into a distant phantom. Light mists arise, and the dew falls, and all the sweet scents in the garden are heavy in the air. Now, the woods settle into great masses[2] as if they were each one profound tree. And now the moon rises, to separate them, and to glimmer here and there in horizontal lines behind their stems, and to make the avenue a pavement of light among high cathedral arches fantastically broken[3].

Now, the moon is high; and the great house, needing habitation more than ever[4], is like a body without life. Now, it is even awful, stealing through it, to think of the live people who have slept in the solitary bedrooms; to say nothing of

---

1. not the first nor the last of beautiful things：= all of the beautiful things
2. masses：轉義為 dark shadows（黑影）。
3. arches fantastically broken：原指拱門奇特地折斷了；但這裏比喻樹幹高大茂密，像拱門羣般，但沒有拱門的對稱，像折斷了的柱一樣。

288

九十三　陰影

　　所有那番景色，從平台上觀望很近。可是，和一切看起來很近，但終歸要變化的美麗的東西一樣，現在正莊嚴地隱沒，變成遠處一片飄渺的幻景。薄霧升起來了，露水下降，空氣裏充溢着花園中濃郁的芬芳氣息。這會兒，樹林變成了大片大片的黑影，彷彿每片黑影就是一棵深邃的大樹。月亮升起來了，把這些黑影分開，從這兒那兒的樹幹後面平射過來，把林蔭道變成明亮的通衢，一條夾在大教堂那些奇異斑駁的高拱門羣中的通衢。

　　明月高升；徹斯尼山莊這幢大房子顯得比任何時候都要孤寂，猶如一個沒有生命的軀殼。現在要是偷偷溜進這所房子去走一圈，想起那些曾經在這些寂寞的臥室裏睡過覺的活人，都會讓人感到毛骨悚然，更不必提那些死人

---

4. needing habitation more than ever：原義 "比任何時候更需要有人
　　居住"；喻指空前的孤寂。這種描寫是從反面來加強正面的效果，襯
　　托出孤寂的程度。

the dead. Now is the time for shadow, when every corner is a cavern, and every downward step a pit, when the stained glass is reflected in pale and faded hues upon the floors, when anything and everything[5] can be made of the heavy staircase beams excepting their own proper shapes, when the armour has dull lights upon it not easily to be distinguished from stealthy movement, and when[6] barred helmets are frightfully suggestive of heads inside. But, of all the shadows in Chesney Wold[7], the shadow in the long drawing-room upon my Lady's picture is the first to come, the last to be disturbed. At this hour and by this light it changes into threatening hands raised up, and menacing the handsome face with every breath that stirs[8].

Charles Dickens: <u>Bleak House</u>

---

5. anything and everything：兩詞都表示"事事"、"一切"的概念。

6. when：在這句以"Now is the time for shadow"開頭的句子中，when一共重複了五次，這種連接詞的故意重複也是一種修辭手法，稱為 polysyndeton，由此引出眾多的平行結構，產生延綿不斷的效果。

7. Wold：山地，高原；此處轉義"建在山上"的大房子。

8. every breath that stirs：每一口氣。

了。這時候，正是陰影大顯神通的時機，每個角落都成了大洞穴，每一級往下的台階都成了陷阱；彩色玻璃在地板上投下暗淡模糊的色彩，一切的東西就好像只有厚實的樓梯橫木，說它們像甚麼都可以，但就不像它們原來的形狀；暗淡的光綫投在盔甲上，就很難辨明到底是盔甲還是有人在偷偷地走動；帶明罩的頭盔看去非常可怕，好像裏面有人的腦袋。可是，在整個切斯尼山莊所有的陰影中，要數那個長長的客廳裏，投射在我夫人肖像上的那個陰影來得最早，走得最晚。這會兒，在月光的照射下，陰影就變成了高舉的可怕的手，一舉一動威脅着夫人那漂亮的面孔。

(英) 狄更斯：《荒涼山莊》

94 The Château

The château, a modern Italian-style building with two projecting wings and three front entrances, was spread out at the far end of an immense lawn on which several cows were grazing among widely spaced clumps of tall trees. Clusters of shrubbery — rhododendrons, syringas and snowballs — lined the curving graveled drive with irregular tufts of verdure. There was a stream flowing under a bridge; through the haze, farm buildings with thatched roofs could be seen scattered over a meadow flanked by two gently sloping wooded hills; at the rear, among dense groups of trees, were two parallel lines of coach houses and stables, remains of the old château which had been torn down.

Gustave Flaubert: Madame Bovary

九十四　法國城堡

　　城堡是座近代意大利風格的建築，兩翼往前突出，正面有三個入口。整幢建築在一大片草坪的盡頭延伸。幾隻母牛在草坪上吃草，在相隔很寬的高樹羣間一簇簇大小不等的灌木——杜鵑花、山梅花、莢蒾、沿着彎彎曲曲的礫石小道，錯落有致地伸展着它們青翠欲滴的枝葉。橋下有一條小溪，透過朦朧霧靄，隱約可見兩座坡度不大，滿山青翠的山崗；中間牧草地上有幾所泥草房頂的農舍。再往裏去，綠蔭翳翳中，車房和馬廄分列兩旁；它們是已經拆毀的舊城堡的殘留部分。

（法）福樓拜：《包法利夫人》

95 Les Trois Couronnes

At the little town of Vevay, in Switzerland, there is a particularly comfortable hotel. There are, indeed, many hotels; for the entertainment of tourists is the business of the place, which, as many travellers will remember, is seated upon the edge of a remarkably blue lake — a lake that it behooves[1] every tourist to visit. The shore of the lake presents an unbroken array of establishments of this order, of every category, from the "grand hotel" of the newest fashion, with a chalk-white front, a hundred balconies, and a dozen flags flying from its roof, to the little Swiss *pension*[2] of an elder day, with its name inscribed in German-looking lettering upon a pink or yellow wall, and an awkward summer-house in the angle of the garden. One of the hotels at Vevay, however, is famous, even classical, being distinguished from any of its upstart neighbors by an air both of luxury and of maturity. In this region, in the month of June, American travellers are extremely numerous; it may be said, indeed,

---

1. behoove：（正式用語）= behove：理應，必須，主語用 it，如："It behooves me to write to him." （我應該給他寫信）。
2. *pension*：法語，歐洲大陸的公寓。

九十五　三冠大酒店

在瑞士的小城鎮——費維，有一家特別舒適的旅館。事實上，那裏有許多家旅館，因為這是一個以旅遊業為主的名勝區。許多到過該地的遊客都會記得，費維坐落在一個藍得十分可愛的湖邊——這個湖是每位遊客必到的地方。各式各樣的旅館沿湖而建，鱗次櫛比，排列成行。從最新穎的大酒店——屋前刷得雪白，有成百個小陽台，屋頂飄着十幾面旗幟——到舊時瑞士的膳宿公寓——這種公寓的名字漆在粉紅色或黃色的牆上，字體略帶德國風味，花園的一角有不倫不類的涼亭——都應有盡有。但是，費維的許多家旅館中，有一家特別出名，堪稱一流。這家旅館以其豪華成熟的氣派令附近那些有暴發戶氣息的旅館相形見絀。每年六月間，總有無數美國遊客來到這裏消夏。

that Vevay assumes at this period some of the characteristics of an American watering-place[3]. There are sights and sounds which evoke a vision, an echo, of Newport[4] and Saratoga[5]. There is a flitting hither and thither of "stylish" young girls, a rustling of muslin flounces, a rattle of dance-music in the morning hours, a sound of high-pitched voices at all times. You receive an impression of these things at the excellent inn of the Trois Couronnes, and are transported in fancy to the Ocean House or to Congress Hall. But at the Trois Couronnes, it must be added, there are other features that are much at variance with these suggestions: neat German waiters, who look like secretaries of legation, Russian princesses sitting in the garden; little Polish boys walking about, held by the hand, with their governors[6]; a view of the sunny crest of the Dent du Midi and the picturesque towers of the Castle of Chillon.

Henry James: <u>Daisy Miller</u>

---

3. watering-place：有沐浴、划船等享受的海濱勝地。
4. Newport：紐波特，美國羅德州東南部一港市，避暑勝地。
5. Saratoga：薩拉托加，美國紐約州東部一市鎮。
6. governors：（英國俚語），父親。

的確，可以這麼說，這時的費維就會呈現出某些美國避暑勝地的特色。那裏的所見所聞時常給人一種印象，彷佛大家又回到了美國的紐波特和薩拉托加。裝束入時的女郎們穿梭於人羣之中，細布衣裙窸窣作響；夜深人靜時陣陣歡鬧的舞曲聲響個不停；一天到晚都能聽得到的高聲喧嚷。這些，在三冠大酒店這家優越的旅館裏都是司空見慣的情景，它總使人想起海洋大廈或國會飯店來。但是，我還要補充説明一下，除了上述特點之外，三冠大酒店還有些迥然不同的特色：那裏有衣冠整潔的德國侍者，看去酷似公使館裏的秘書；俄羅斯的公主們坐在園裏休憩；波蘭小男孩們攙着爸爸的手，在園中散步。從酒店眺望遠處，又可以看得見唐・杜・米迪山頂陽光絢爛的景色，還有希龍古堡那些如詩如畫的塔樓。

（美）亨利・詹姆士：《黛西・米勒》

96   A Steel Bridge of a Single Span

The late afternoon sun that still came over the brown shoulder of the mountain showed the bridge dark against the steep emptiness of the gorge. It was a steel bridge of a single span and there was a sentry box at each end. It was wide enough for two motor cars to pass and it spanned, in solid-flung metal grace, a deep gorge at the bottom of which, far below, a brook leaped in white water[1] through rocks and boulders down to the main stream of the pass.

The sun was in Robert Jordan's eyes and the bridge showed only in outline. Then the sun lessened and was gone and looking up through the trees at the brown, rounded height that it had gone behind, he saw, now, that he no longer looked into the glare[2], that the mountain slope was a delicate new green and that there were patches of old snow under the crest.

Ernest Hemingway: <u>For Whom the Bell Tolls</u>

---

1. white water：浪花。
2. looked into the glare：直視刺眼的陽光。

九十六　單孔鐵橋

　　夕陽仍然越過褐色的山肩，照了過來，在峽谷前那陡峭的空間的映襯下，那座鐵橋顯得黑魆魆的。那是一座單孔鐵橋，橋的兩端各有一個崗亭，橋面很寬，可以同時並行兩輛汽車。這座堅固的鐵橋綫條優美，橫跨在峽谷上，下面深深的谷底有一條白浪飛濺的小溪，流過礁石和巨礫，奔向山口那邊的主流。

　　陽光正對着羅伯特·喬丹的眼睛，眼前的橋只現出一個剪影。陽光漸漸地減弱，暗了下來，最後，夕陽終於落了下去。這時，他透過樹林眺望這座太陽沉落的圓滾滾的褐色山頭，不再感到眩目，展現在他眼前的是遍地青翠的山坡，山峯下還有一堆一堆的殘雪。

（美）海明威：《戰地鐘聲》

97   Broadway

The walk down Broadway, then as now, was one of the remarkable features of the city. There gathered, before the matinée[1] and afterwards, not only all the pretty women who love a showy parade, but the men who love to gaze upon and admire them. It was a very imposing procession of pretty faces and fine clothes. Women appeared in their very best hats, shoes, and gloves, and walked arm in arm on their way to the fine shops or theatres strung along from Fourteenth to Thirty-fourth streets. Equally the men paraded with the very latest[2] they could afford. A tailor might have secured hints on suit measurements, a shoemaker on proper lasts[3] and colours, a hatter on hats. It was literally true that if a lover of fine clothes secured a new suit, it was sure to have its first airing[4] on Broadway. So true and well understood was this fact, that several years later a popular song, detailing this and other facts concerning the afternoon parade on matinée days, and entitled "What Right Has He on Broadway?" was published, and had quite a vogue about the music-halls of the city.

---

1. matinée：（法語詞彙）午後的演出，日戲。
2. the very latest ＝ the latest fashion；指最時髦的服飾。

九十七　百老匯街景

　　在百老匯街上散步，過去和現在一樣，是這個城市生活中的一大特色。在日戲開場前和散場後，那裏不僅有成羣結隊的愛賣弄姿色的美麗婦人，也有許多愛看女人，羨慕美女的男人。這是由靚女們的俏麗臉蛋和華麗服飾組成的壯觀的行列，女人們都用最漂亮的帽子、鞋子和手套打扮起來，臂挽着臂，漫步在第十四街到三十四街的大街上，在大商場或劇院裏進進出出。男人們也一樣，炫耀着他們買得起的最時髦的服裝。從這裏，裁縫或許可以得到些關於裁剪的最新啟迪；鞋匠了解到甚麼鞋型和顏色最流行；帽匠會明白甚麼式樣最時髦。這是千真萬確的，一個講究服飾的人置了一套新裝，是一定會首先在百老匯路上亮相，這幾乎是盡人皆知的事。幾年之後，還出版了一首流行歌曲，詳細描述在那些時興看日戲的日子裏的風光場面，曲名叫"他憑甚麼到百老匯來？"當時在紐約的音樂廳裏還着實風行了一陣。

3.　lasts：鞋楦。

4.　airing：顯示，炫耀。

In all her stay in the city, Carrie had never heard of this showy parade; had never even been on Broadway when it was taking place. On the other hand, it was a familiar thing to Mrs. Vance, who not only knew of it as an entity, but had often been in it, going purposely to see and be seen, to create a stir with her beauty and dispel any tendency to fall short in dressiness by contrasting herself with the beauty and fashion of the town.

Carrie stepped along easily enough after they got out of the car at Thirty-fourth Street, but soon fixed her eyes upon the lovely company which swarmed by and with them as they proceeded. She noticed suddenly that Mrs. Vance's manner had rather stiffened under the gaze of handsome men and elegantly dressed ladies, whose glances were not modified by any rules of propriety[5]. To stare seemed the proper and natural thing. Carrie found herself stared at and ogled. Men in flawless top-coats, high hats, and silver-headed walking sticks elbowed near and looked too often into conscious eyes. Ladies rustled by in dresses of stiff cloth, shedding affected smiles and perfume. Carrie noticed among

---

5. whose glances were not modified by any rules of propriety：rule of propriety 是禮儀。這裏指那些人盯着凡斯太太，絲毫不受禮儀束縛，也即是不顧禮貌地望着她。

嘉莉在城裏住了這麼久，還從未風聞過這個大出風頭的場面；當百老匯的美女雲集的時候，她還從未去過那區。相反，凡斯太太是慣於此道的，她不僅知道它的存在，而且常常置身其間。故意去看看，或者讓人看看，以她的美貌去製造一種轟動效應，跟城裏的美女們爭艷鬥俏，以免自己的服飾打扮有任何落伍於時尚的苗頭。

在三十四街下車之後，嘉莉輕鬆自在地跟着凡斯太太走去，但眼光很快就落在和她們一起走着的熙來攘往、成羣結隊的美人兒身上。她突然發覺一些裝束入時的俊男美女們，用毫不掩飾的目光注視着凡斯太太，使她的神情變得十分局促。盯住看似乎是應該的、自然的事。嘉莉發現也有人在端詳她，給她送秋波。身穿完美的精品大衣，戴禮帽，手執銀頭手杖的男士擦肩而過，常常故意朝她那雙敏感的眼睛望上一眼。身着高級裙服的女士們從旁而過，香氣撲鼻，衣裙窸窣作響，流露出喬模喬樣的微笑。在其

them the sprinkling of goodness and the heavy percentage of vice[6]. The rouged and powdered cheeks and lips, the scented hair, the large, misty, and languorous eye, were common enough. With a start she awoke to find that she was in fashion's crowd, on parade in a show place — and such a show place! Jewellers' windows gleamed along the path with remarkable frequency. Florist shops, furriers, haberdashers[7], confectioners — all followed in rapid succession. The street was full of coaches. Pompous doormen in immense[8] coats, shiny brass belts and buttons, waited in front of expensive salesrooms. Coachmen in tan boots, white tights, and blue jackets waited obsequiously for the mistresses of carriages who were shopping inside. The whole street bore the flavour of riches and show, and Carrie felt that she was not of it. She could not, for the life of her[9], assume the attitude and smartness of Mrs. Vance, who, in her beauty, was all assurance. She could only imagine that it must be evident to

---

6. the sprinkling of goodness and the heavy percentage of vice：少少的善意，多多的邪氣。
7. haberdashers：（美國用語）男士服飾用品店。
8. immense：（口語）好極的。
9. for the life of her：無論如何也……；要她的命也……。

間，嘉莉注意到她們的微笑在友善中存着不少邪氣。到處都是塗脂抹粉的臉蛋和嘴唇，噴灑了香水的頭髮，迷離、懶洋洋的大眼睛。她突然吃驚地發現，她自己是在麗人行列之中，置身於時裝展覽的場所——而且是那樣地招人眼目的地方！沿街隨處都是珠寶商店的櫥窗，鮮花舖、皮草店、男士服飾用品店、糖果店—— 一家挨着一家。街上車水馬龍，昂貴商店的門口站着身穿極漂亮的外衣、腰圍發亮的銅帶和銅釦，氣派不凡的看門人；穿着褐色長統皮靴，白色緊身衣褲和藍色短上衣的馬車夫，諂媚地等待着在店裏購物的女主人。整條街道都洋溢着富麗堂皇及炫耀的色調。嘉莉覺得自己是個局外人，自覺一輩子也不可能擁有凡斯太太這份儀態和風雅，而打扮美艷的凡斯太太是萬無一失的。她只能這樣想，在許多人的眼裏，她顯然是

many that she was the less handsomely dressed of the two. It cut her to the quick, and she resolved that she would not come here again until she looked better. At the same time she longed to feel the delight of parading here as an equal. Ah, then she would be happy!

Theodore Dreiser: <u>Sister Carrie</u>

兩人中服飾打扮較遜色的一個；這立即刺痛了她的心，就決定要是以後不打扮得更漂亮一些就不上這兒來。與此同時，她又渴望着能跟凡斯太太一樣，打扮得漂漂亮亮的，好到這裏來出一下風頭，稱稱她的心。啊！那樣她就幸福了。

（美）德萊塞：《嘉莉妹妹》

98 Camping

And then that evening at sundown, on the west shore of this same lake, on an open sward[1] that was as smooth as any well-kept lawn, the entire company settled, in five different colored tents ranged about a fire like an Indian village, with cooks' and servants' tents in the distance. And the half dozen canoes beached like bright fish along the grassy shore of the lake. And then supper around an open fire. And Baggott and Harriet and Stuart and Grant, after furnishing music for the others to dance by, organizing by the flare of a large gasoline lamp, a poker game. And the others joining in singing ribald[2] camping and college songs, no one of which Clyde knew, yet in which he tried to join. And shouts of laughter. And bets as to who would be the first to catch the first fish, to shoot the first squirrel or partridge, to win the first race. And lastly, solemn plans for moving the camp at least ten miles farther east, after breakfast, on the morrow[3] where was an ideal beach, and where they would be within five miles of

---

1. sward ：草皮，帶草的地面。
2. ribald ：下流的。
3. morrow：（古語）＝ morning 或 the next day。

九十八　野營風光

　　在夕陽西下的薄暮時分，全隊人馬在同一個湖的西岸
一片空曠的草地上紮營寨。草地平滑得如同任何保養得很
好的草坪一般，五個色彩各異的帳篷圍着火堆而建，就像
印第安人的村落一樣，廚師和傭人的帳篷離得遠些。六條
獨木舟宛如六條白閃閃的魚，躺在長了草的湖岸邊。然後
大家圍着露天的營火吃晚飯。巴格特·哈里特·斯圖爾特和
格蘭特準備好給別人伴舞的樂曲，便在一盞大型煤氣燈的
燈光旁安排了一局撲克遊戲。其他人紛紛唱起了粗獷的野
營歌曲和校園歌曲。克萊德連一支歌也不會唱，但他還是
盡量隨聲附和一番。還有那一陣陣大笑，還有打賭：看誰
釣得第一條魚，射中第一隻松鼠或鷗鴣，在頭一次競賽中
划得最快。最後，是鄭重其事的計劃，打算明日早餐後，
把帳篷至少向東推移十哩路。那裏有一片理想的湖灘，離

the Metissic Inn, and where they could dine and dance to their heart's content.

And then the silence and the beauty of this camp at night, after all had presumably gone to bed. The stars! The mystic, shadowy water, faintly rippling in a light wind, the mystic, shadowy pines conferring[4] in the light breezes, the cries of night birds and owls — too disturbing to Clyde to be listened to with anything but inward distress.

...

But then the glory of the morning once more — with its rotund and yellow sun rising over the waters of the lake — and in a cove across the lake wild ducks padding about. And after a time Grant and Stuart and Harley, half-clad and with guns and a great show of fowling skill, foolishly setting forth in canoes in the hope of bagging[5] some of the game with long-distance shots, yet getting nothing, to the merriment of all the others. And the boys and girls, stealing out in bright-colored bathing suits and silken beach robes to the water,

---

4. conferring：原義 "傾談，交換看法" ；這裏指在微風吹動下，松林沙沙作響，猶如人在談話。
5. bagging：捕殺鳥獸等，獵獲。

梅蒂西克旅館只有五哩路,他們就可以盡情地吃喝,痛快地跳舞了。

夜晚來臨,所有的人該都沉入了夢鄉,營地上一片寂靜,有多美!那星星啊!那神秘、幽暗的湖水,在微風中掀起陣陣漣漪;那些神秘、幽暗的松樹隨着微風沙沙低吟;還有那些夜鳥和貓頭鷹的叫聲,在內心痛苦不堪的克萊德聽來都覺得難以忍受

……

在這之後,瑰麗的清晨再次降臨人間,圓圓的、黃澄澄的太陽從湖面上冉冉升起。湖對岸的小水灣裏,野鴨在水中嬉戲。隔了一會兒,格蘭特,斯圖爾特和哈里連衣服也未及穿整齊,便提着槍,顯出一付自以為是獵野禽的高手的神情,傻裏傻氣地乘着獨木船出發了,滿心希望用遠距離射擊,獵幾隻野禽回來,結果卻一無所獲,倒把其他人都逗得樂不可支。還有那些男孩、女孩們,穿上了色彩艷麗的游泳衣和絲綢海灘裙裝,輕手輕腳地走出去,然後

there to plunge gayly in and shout and clatter[6] concerning the joy of it all. And breakfast at nine, with afterwards the gayety[7] and beauty of the bright flotilla of canoes making eastward along the southern lake shore, banjos, guitars and mandolins strumming and voices raised in song, jest, laughter.

Theodore Dreiser: <u>An American Tragedy</u>

---

6. clatter：喧鬧，高聲談論。
7. gayety ＝ gaiety

興高采烈地撲到水裏，高聲喊啊，叫啊，嘰嘰呱呱談論着玩樂的事。九點吃早飯，飯後一小隊亮閃閃的獨木船沿着南邊湖岸向東划，一時間，五彩繽紛，喜氣洋洋。此時，班卓琴、吉他、曼陀林，都一齊奏了起來，**陣陣歌聲**，嬉鬧聲，歡笑聲，一浪高似一浪。

（美）德萊塞：《美國的悲劇》

99   A Valley of Ashes[1]

About half way between West Egg and New York the motor road hastily joins the railroad and runs beside it for a quarter of a mile, so as to shrink away from a certain desolate area of land. This is a valley of ashes — a fantastic farm where ashes grow like wheat into ridges and hills and grotesque gardens; where ashes take the forms of houses and chimneys and rising smoke and, finally, with a transcendent effort, of ash-gray men who move dimly and already crumbling through the powdery air. Occasionally a line of gray cars crawls along an invisible track, gives out a ghastly creak, and comes to rest, and immediately the ash-gray men swarm up with leaden spades and stir up an impenetrable cloud, which screens their obscure operations from your sight.

F.S. Fitzgerald: The Great Gatsby

---

1. A Valley of Ashes：灰燼谷，指堆放灰渣的垃圾場，它位於繁華的紐約市與高級住宅區之間。這不僅是一種對比，更是一種影射，點出了繁華生活的實質。正因為它的強烈象徵意義，作者一度曾想把小說取名為 *Among the Ash-Heaps and Millionaires*。

九十九　灰爐谷

　　紐約和西卵之間大約一半路程的地方，汽車路匆匆匯
上了鐵路，在它旁邊跑上約四分之一哩，為的是要躲開一
處荒涼的地方。這是一個灰爐的山谷——一個離奇古怪的
農場，在這裏，灰爐像麥子一樣生長，長成小山小丘和奇
形怪狀的園子；這裏的灰爐堆得像房子，煙囱和升騰的煙
霧，最後，經過超常的力量，堆成一個個灰蒙蒙的人。他
們在隱隱約約地走動，而且已經在塵土飛揚的空氣中倒了
下來。偶爾一列灰色的貨車沿着一條看不見的鐵軌爬了過
來，發出嘎吱一聲鬼叫，停了下來。那些灰蒙蒙的人拖着
鉛灰色的鐵鏟，一窩蜂似地擁了上來，揚起一片厚厚的塵
土，讓你看不到他們的隱秘活動。

　　　　　（美）菲茨傑拉德：《了不起的蓋茨比》

100 The View of the Battlefield

Looking before him as he mounted the steps of the approach to the knoll, Pierre was spellbound[1] by the beauty of the scene. It was the same panorama he had admired the day before, but now the entire region was covered with troops and clouds of smoke from the guns, and in the clear morning air the slanting rays of the bright sun, which was rising slightly to the left behind Pierre, suffused it with a rosy, golden light streaked with long dark shadows. The distant forests that enclosed the panorama seemed carved out of some precious stone of a yellowish-green color; its undulating contour[2], silhouetted against the horizon, was intersected beyond Valuyevo by the Smolensk highway, now crowded with troops. In the foreground shimmered golden fields and thickets. Everywhere — in front and to the right and left — there were troops. The whole scene was vivid, majestic, and astounding, but what impressed Pierre most was the view of the battlefield itself, of Borodino, and the ravines on either side of the Kolocha.

Over the river, over Borodino and on both sides of it —

---

1. spellbound ：被迷惑；spell ：魔咒。

一百　戰火中的原野

　　皮埃爾順着通道的階梯登上小山丘，他朝前面望去，眼前的美景讓他着了迷。這還是他昨天欣賞過的同一幅全景，可是，現在這一片地方全被軍隊和硝煙所湮沒。明亮的太陽從皮埃爾身後左方升起，斜射的光綫透過清晨潔淨的空氣，在這幅全景畫上投下一道玫瑰色，金色的光綫和長長的黑影。遠處全景邊沿的樹林彷彿是用某種黃綠色的寶石雕刻出來的；樹林在天際顯出了蜿蜒起伏的輪廓，並在伏盧亞佛村後和斯摩林斯克大道相交。大道上全是軍隊，前面周圍是閃閃發亮的金色的田野和樹叢。前面、右面和左面，到處都是軍隊，整個景色呈現出一片栩栩如生的壯觀景象，令人吃驚。但給皮埃爾印象最深的是戰場本身的景象，即波羅帝諾和考洛查河兩岸的峽谷的景象。

　　在考洛查河上，在波羅帝諾村和河的兩岸，尤其是在

2.　contour：輪廓綫。

especially to the left where the Voyna flowed through marshy land and fell into the Kolocha — hung a mist that spread, dissolved, and grew translucent in the brilliant sunlight, magically tinting and outlining everything seen through it. The smoke of the guns mingled with this mist, and everywhere glints of morning light sparkled through it, now on the water, now on the dew, now on the bayonets of the soldiers crowded along the riverbanks and in Borodino. A white church could be seen through the mist, here and there a cottage roof, dense masses of troops, green caissons, cannons. And all was in motion, or appeared to move, as the smoke and mist drifted over the whole landscape. Just as in the mist-covered hollows near Borodino, so along the entire line beyond and above it, and especially to the left, in woods and meadows, over valleys and on ridges, clouds of cannon smoke seemed to materialize out of nothing, now singly, now several at a time, now sparse, now dense, expanding, billowing, merging, swirling over the whole expanse.

These puffs of smoke and, strange to say, the reports[3] that accompanied them, produced the chief beauty of the spectacle.

Lev Tolstoy: War and Peace

---

3. reports：爆炸聲，射擊聲。

左岸，在伏耶那河穿越過沼澤流入考洛查河的地方，彌漫
着一層霧氣，霧逐漸地擴散，消失，在燦爛的陽光照射下
變成半透明。透過薄霧見到的樣樣事物都像加上了輪廓，
並像給塗上了一層魔幻般的色彩。硝煙和霧混雜着，在霧
裏和煙裏，到處都閃現出微弱的晨光，有的在水面上，有
的在露珠兒上，有的在擁擠在波羅帝諾河兩岸的士兵們的
刺刀上。透過這層霧可以看到白色的教堂，這裏那裏的小
屋的屋頂，密集的軍隊，綠色的彈藥箱和大炮。煙和霧在
這整個原野飄蕩着，一切都在運動之中，或者像是在移
動。跟波羅帝諾附近的低窪處被霧所籠罩一樣，外邊整個
沿綫和沿綫上空情形也都一樣。尤其是在左面，在樹林裏
和草地上，在山谷和山脊的上空，大炮的煙雲彷彿憑空冒
了出來，有時是單獨的一股，有時同時冒出好幾股，時淡
時濃。硝煙緩緩升騰，時而擴散，時而混合，在整片地域
繚繞不定。

說來也怪，這陣陣硝煙和伴隨的槍砲聲，竟然是這片
景觀主要美麗之處。

（俄）列夫·托爾斯泰：《戰爭與和平》

外國名著風景描寫一百段 = 100 scenic
descriptions from great novels ／ 張合珍選
譯. -- 臺灣初版. -- 臺北市：臺灣商務，
1997〔民86〕
　　面　；　公分. -- (一百叢書；19)
　　ISBN 957-05-1361-6 (平裝)

813.6　　　　　　　　　　　　85013131

一百叢書 ⑲

外國名著風景描寫一百段
100 SCENIC DESCRIPTIONS
FROM GREAT NOVELS

定價新臺幣 320 元

選 譯 者	張 合 珍	
編 審 者	張 信 威	
責任編輯	金 堅	
發 行 人	王 學 哲	

出 版 者
印 刷 所　臺灣商務印書館股份有限公司
　　　　　臺北市 10036 重慶南路 1 段 37 號
　　　　　電話：(02)23116118 ・ 23115538
　　　　　傳眞：(02)23710274 ・ 23701091
　　　　　讀者服務專線：0800056196
　　　　　E-mail:cptw@ms12.hinet.net
　　　　　網址：www.cptw.com.tw
　　　　　郵政劃撥：0000165 － 1 號
出版事業
登 記 證：局版北市業字第 993 號

・ 1996 年 8 月香港初版
・ 1997 年 2 月臺灣初版第一次印刷
・ 2005 年 4 月臺灣初版第三次印刷
本書經商務印書館（香港）有限公司授權出版

ISBN　957-05-1361-6（平裝）　　　　b 26247000

一百叢書　100 SERIES

英漢・漢英對照